BLOOD TIES

THE SEARCHERS
BOOK ONE

JESSICA MARTING

SHADOW PRESS

BLOOD TIES

Blood Ties (The Searchers Book 1)

ISBN 978-1-989780-25-1

Copyright © 2016, 2023 J.L. Turner

Second Edition

This book was previously published by Evernight Publishing. It has been expanded and re-edited.

Cover art by German Creative

For David, of course.

CHAPTER
ONE

Dear Mr. Sterling,
    I assure you that despite the date this missive was written, this is not a grotesque April Fools' Day prank, nor were the other letters and telegrams I and your uncle's solicitor also sent over the previous three months, which you have also ignored. In the event that you haven't received them, I repeat their contents: your uncle James has moved on to the next world, and under strange circumstances. I urge you to abandon your gallivanting about the continent and return to London to at least see to your late uncle's affairs, if not re-settle here permanently.

    As I have written before and will reiterate now, I am fully prepared to continue on my work as butler of your uncle's home. It, and I, are awaiting your arrival. Please send word as soon as possible.

    Yours sincerely,
    Silas Weston

❧

THE LETTER from his late uncle's butler burned a hole in his pocket, but Maximilian Sterling would not be denied a little pleasantry during his last hours in Paris. It wasn't his first visit to the *la ville lumière*, although this occasion marked the first time he saw the Eiffel Tower since its completion. It also didn't hurt that he had a lovely companion with whom to enjoy his final supper in France, one who spoke nearly fluent English as well.

Lisette beamed at him from across the table, her face and golden hair illuminated by the hotel's gas lamps. "Our meeting is such a lovely coincidence," she purred. She took a delicate sip from the wine glass in her hand.

Max nodded, unable to keep the smile from his face. It was refreshing to meet someone who spoke to him without waiting to be introduced first, who could keep up with him when he said he wanted to climb as many stairs of the Tower as he was allowed. Her happening to also be booked on the same London-bound dirigible he was tonight was a happy coincidence.

"It is," he said. "Although I *am* disappointed in your refusal of my offer."

A look of mock outrage crossed her features. "*Monsieur* Sterling!" She gasped. "You know it would not be proper for me to do so. I know even widows cannot stay in the house of an unmarried Englishman!" The twinkle didn't leave her eyes, but he knew Lisette meant her words. Her stay in London would be spent in a hotel.

The mention of England sent a twinge of regret through him. Once again, the folded letter from Silas Weston weighed heavily on his mind. He wasn't returning to London because he wanted to; his blasted uncle had gone and died on him, leaving him with a musty old house in a country he didn't care for.

Lisette was still waiting for a reply, so he forced a smile to his face. "Of course," he said. "I'm merely enjoying scandalous conversation while I still can."

"You English worry too much about your manners," Lisette said. "I suppose I will have to remember that while I am visiting."

They had met at the base of the Eiffel Tower only two hours prior, just after dark settled over Paris. Lisette's reasons for leaving France were still a little unclear, although Max hadn't been exactly forthcoming about his reasons for leaving, either. He wouldn't think about it, not until the dirigible touched ground in London. All he knew about Lisette was that she was from Paris and a widow, her husband having been gone long enough so that she no longer wore mourning. "I hope you will still agree to sharing supper with me some evening," he said. At her raised eyebrow, he added, "At your hotel, in the public eating area. I understand the cuisine at the Langham Hotel is unsurpassed." He didn't, as he preferred to stay in his own rented rooms on the rare occasions he was in London, but he didn't mention that to Lisette.

His uncle's death left him saddled with a big, empty house to return to and take care of in a country where it never seemed to stop raining. The mere thought of it filled him with cold dread.

Lisette pushed her mostly-uneaten dessert a few inches away and took another sip from her wine glass. Strange, she'd only picked at her supper, but the glass and a half of Bordeaux she'd enjoyed instead didn't appear to have any effect on her. "We should make our way to the dirigible," she said. "It leaves shortly."

A quick glance at his watch told Max that their time in the restaurant had gone by much more quickly than he realized, and they had less than an hour before their dirigible left. He quickly settled the bill. Once in the street with Lisette, he escorted her into one of the steam-powered cabs waiting outside the hotel.

His hope for an evening of conversation and wine with her evaporated. His unease returned, lodging itself as a ball in the pit of his stomach as he thought of his impending return to London.

"DAMN IT."

Ada didn't know what irritated her the most: that her target was escaping in a cab, that her French was so poor, that she was running low on funds, or that Lisette Babineau was so frustratingly wily. It was equally irritating, she decided, as she tossed her much-repaired satchel over her shoulder and ran for a cab. Or tried to run; her boots and corset weren't conducive to such exercises. She had to pawn a great deal of her belongings after she ran out of money in Switzerland, so at least the satchel wasn't too heavy. She wished blending in wasn't so uncomfortable when she was hunting.

She threw herself into the back seat of the steam-powered cab before ordering the startled driver to follow the two vehicles ahead. "As quickly as you can," she said, noting the wince on the driver's face at her accent. It made Ada cringe, too, and hope that wherever her mark and her unlucky companion were going, it wouldn't be too expensive. She needed to return to New York and her version of normalcy as soon as possible, for her own sanity. She had long since given up on the hope of returning to Germany to complete her much-needed holiday.

The driver grumbled about *idiot Américains*, but followed Madame Babineau's cab through the gas-lit streets of Paris to an airfield. Ada was immediately disappointed at the thought of spending more money on an dirigible ticket, but on the upside, her target wouldn't be able to escape so easily. While vampires could fly or shift into bats, her boarding a dirigible meant she probably didn't intend to pull off such a stunt.

"*Merci.*" She paid the driver and let herself out of the cab without another word. The driver shot her a dirty look and drove away, steam issuing from the vehicle's vents.

Madame Babineau and her friend took places in the queue for first class passengers. Ada took her place in line for deck class, keeping her eye on the vampire from beneath her hat brim. She wondered where this dirigible would take her, if she would have enough time to stake the vampire and dispose of her ashes before the journey was over.

When it was her turn at the queue, she smiled as nicely as she could manage and said, "*Un billet, sil vous plaît.*"

"*Aller retour?*" the clerk asked. *Return trip?*

Ada didn't have any intention of returning to France. "*Non.* One way, if you please."

The ticket the man sold her was stamped *Londres/London*. Well, that was a bit of a relief. She would only have to worry about stuffy etiquette and stuffier people than trying to speak the language. She doubted she would have enough time to

5

handle Madame Babineau onboard, but she would tail the vampire until she found an opportunity to stake her. She might even have enough time to do a little sightseeing. It wouldn't make up for her aborted trip to Dresden, but it might mean that her time overseas wasn't a complete wash.

The dirigible was a small one, meant for short journeys, and didn't have any passenger berths, just big common areas. Her ticket entitled her to a spot on a bench on the dirigible's deck, under a wide awning. The first class passengers' compartment was covered and probably heated, if its windows fogging up from bodies and the spring chill outside was any indication. Of course its well-heeled occupants didn't give any notice of the passengers outside, Ada thought irritably. She tugged her coat around her a little more tightly and slipped on her gloves, which she hadn't had to wear since her trip to Bern two weeks prior. She'd managed to stake a vampire who escaped her in Berlin, but it had been … messy. Her gloves were still stained with greasy ash. *Ugh*, she thought, looking down at the ruined material.

Through the first class compartment windows ahead of her, she spotted Lisette Babineau and her companion, getting a good look at him for the first time. Ada's heart sped up a little at the sight. Damn, but he was a handsome man, and exactly the sort she tended to go for: tall, broad-shouldered, dark hair and eyes. Judging from the cut of his coat—obviously not a ready-made garment, either—he looked firm, a rarity in Europe's upper classes, Ada had noted over her time there. She hoped Madame Babineau didn't eat him or, worse, turn him, before Ada could introduce herself.

Forget Big Ben. A few hours with the man

would be all the memories of merry old England she wanted.

Through the foggy glass, the vampire looked up abruptly, the smile on her beautiful face wiped away. She looked over the crowd in the first class compartment, scanning their faces. Ada quickly leaned down, pretending to inspect her boot, and re-tied its lace to give herself some more time. Dhampir-descended Searchers could sense vampires, but most vampires could not sense Searchers. It was impossible to know which ones could, as it was an unusual talent for vampires. Unusual, and frightening. There were fewer Searchers than vampires, and it was vital to keep their identities and headquarters secret.

She kept her head down until the dirigible lifted off. Ada crossed her arms and stuffed her hands in her armpits to ward off the cold, guessing it was only going to get worse when they started over the English Channel. She was right. It was cold, miserable, and unfortunately for the poor bastards strapped to benches outside, starting to drizzle. When she looked up, she saw the vampire and the man accepting glasses of wine from a liveried footman. The suspicious look was gone from the vampire's face. Ada discreetly kept her eye on the couple through the window the entire journey, tuning out her fellow passengers and ignoring hawkers selling watery tea and hard tack-type biscuits.

The trip was over seventy-five miserable moments later, and Ada was the first passenger out of her seat and down the gangplank. Once back on land, she waited for her quarry to disembark.

They were among the last to leave the dirigible, laughing gaily at something. One of the electric lamps that threw light over the airfield sizzled and burned out as they passed beneath it, but Ada wasn't deterred. Pushing her satchel over her shoulder, she kept at a discreet distance and followed them.

Night was rapidly falling and with it, an urge to go out and find what amusements, if any, London had on offer. He wanted to do anything but go into his late uncle's mausoleum of a house, Max thought, then quickly pushed it away. Uncle James's passing would *not* be something he would dwell on tonight. He had a lovely, charming woman at his side and he wasn't yet ready to leave her.

But Lisette's demeanour changed when they slipped into a steam-powered cab. The vehicles in London were newer than their Parisian counterparts, and the cab nearly sailed over the street in the direction of the Langham Hotel. She craned her neck and looked through the cab's small, round rear mirror. "Is everything all right?" Max asked. "You seem nervous."

She faced him, an overly bright smile pasted on her face. "Of course," she said. "I am simply not used to England. The vehicles are so much faster." She turned around and squinted at the dark road again.

Were they being followed? Max also turned around, but saw nothing except carriages and steam cabs behind them. "Shall I expect a fight later on in the evening?" he asked, trying to keep his tone light.

She turned back to him, the light from the gas

lamps outside showing the irritation flashing across her elfin features. "*Non*," she replied. Her eyes darted back to the road for a second before meeting his. "I apologize, Max. I am simply tired. I hadn't expected to meet you or climb the *Tour d'Eiffel* tonight."

Max was used to long journeys and little sleep, and it was easy to forget that most people weren't accustomed to as much exertion as he was. Lisette had remarkably kept up with him, so it shouldn't be a surprise for her to be tired.

The bright street lamps of Regent Street greeted them, splattered lightly with rain. When the cab stopped in front of the Langham Hotel, Max quickly paid the driver before getting out to help Lisette from the vehicle. She looked up at the building, and then smiled at him.

"I think you should visit me tonight," she said.

Max's eyes widened in surprise, but he wasn't about to turn down the offer. "Are you certain?" he asked.

She nodded. "Just for a few moments."

Max offered her his arm and tried to inject just the right amount of suggestion into his voice. "My dear, I'll need more than a few moments."

LISETTE'S ROOMS were waiting for her, as well as a pair of trunks that must have been sent before they boarded the dirigible to London. She turned on a few lamps, throwing yellow light over the luxuriously-appointed room, and gave him a sly smile as she draped her coat over the back of a chair.

"You must think me terribly of me," she said. She opened a bottle of wine left on a table, pouring some into a pair of glasses. She pouted at the room, at her coat, then sighed. "No lady's maid. I will have to see about that later tonight." She held out a wine glass to him.

More wine? While Max was an adventurer, even he couldn't spend a day and night drinking, if only due to the boredom it would eventually bring on. He preferred his mind to be as sharp as possible. "I have to decline," he said.

She frowned before taking a generous sip from her glass. "Please, I insist."

Why not? Max knew he wouldn't be getting any writing in tonight, so he may as well indulge. He would enjoy one more glass of wine and a romp with Lisette, and … then what? Go to the flat he maintained for such visits? Go to his uncle's house? Both options were too lonely to consider.

His hand clenched around the glass, only relaxing when Lisette touched it. "I would like a toast."

"Of course. To new friends." Max met her eyes, clinked his glass to hers.

But there was something strange about Lisette's eyes. They bored into him, a gaze he could physically feel. His head grew heavy, his body felt bolted to the floor. He tried to look away, but found he couldn't.

"I apologize, Max," Lisette said, but her voice sounded far away. The air grew thicker, and it became harder to breathe.

"What?" He barely managed to get the word out. Dimly, he was aware of his hand relaxing and his glass slipping out, wine splashing across the pristine carpet.

"You are a very nice man," she said, but her voice sounded garbled behind the pair of fangs that now extended over her lips. She leaned toward his neck, breathing deeply. "You smell divine."

Fangs? That was impossible.

"I see you're not completely under my thrall," she said softly. "I apologize for that, too, because it will hurt."

Max still couldn't move, not even when she jumped up and sank her fangs into his neck.

CHAPTER
TWO

Ada mentally tallied the amount of money she was going to demand from the Searchers as soon as she returned to New York. After bribing a clerk to find out Madame Babineau's room number at this gilded monstrosity of a hotel, she was officially out of money. At the very least, she would have to dig through the vampire's personal effects and hope she had a few pounds on her to get her through the rest of this trip.

She took an ornate elevator to the vampire's top floor room, ignoring the way her stomach flip-flopped at its movements. No wonder everyone here was so soft, she thought, looking at the elevator operator and the other passengers. They spent as much time as they could thinking up ways to avoid straining their bodies. It wasn't healthy.

Except for that Englishman, she remembered. Who could very well be the vampire's evening snack about now.

That thought spurred her to the front of the elevator car, and she was the first one out, walking as quickly as she could to the last room on the floor, a corner one. All those windows would make it more difficult to make the room light-tight, but if Madame Babineau had had enough of a meal beforehand, a little sunlight through the curtains might not be a problem for her. Ada had never stopped wishing that vampires were as vulnerable to sunlight as they were purported to be. It would make her job so much easier.

As she tiptoed along the corridor's plush carpet, she retrieved a silver necklace with a cross dangling from it and an icepick from her bag. The cross went around her neck; the icepick was looped over one finger. Then she withdrew a short, sharpened stake and mallet from her bag, tucking them under her arm.

She pressed her ear against the door and heard a surprised yell, followed by a distinctive hiss only vampires could make.

Damn it! She jammed the icepick in the door's keyhole and wiggled it around desperately, pushing against the knob with her other hand until the door swung open. She nearly fell into the room and slammed the door behind her.

Lisette Babineau looked up, her fangs still embedded in the Englishman's throat. Judging from the look of terror on his face, he hadn't been enthralled first, either. He fought against her, muscles straining in his well-cut coat, but even a young vampire was stronger than a human man.

The vampire snarled at Ada, blood running down her chin. The vampire let out a garbled scream, followed by, "*Casse-toi!*" The man staggered back, his hand reaching for his throat to staunch the flow of blood, and landed in an ornate overstuffed chair.

Ada did *not* care for a vampire telling her to fuck off.

Madame Babineau hadn't had time to seal the wound she'd opened on the man's throat, and he pressed the vampire's discarded shawl against it, his eyes never leaving Ada's face. "Give me a minute," Ada said.

She sprang into action, splashing holy water in Madame Babineau's face. The vampire screamed as her skin sizzled, and Ada shoved the small vial back in her pocket. Madame Babineau clawed at her smoking face, giving Ada the chance to leap the few inches separating them and plunge her stake into the vampire's heart.

Shock bloomed across her face, and she sank to her knees, heavy skirts bloodstained and in disarray. She turned hateful, ruined eyes to Ada. "*Putain!*" she snarled. Her eyes rolled up in the back of her head, and she disintegrated into a pile of greasy dust and expensive fabric.

The Englishman's rapid, panicked breathing had Ada turning around. She took a few steps closer to him, but he shrank back in his chair, clutching the shawl against his throat. "Get away from me," he croaked.

"You should've said that to Lisette Babineau back in Paris. Let me take a look at that." She reached for the shawl, but he stumbled to his feet, eyes glued to the oily remains of the French vampire.

"What the *hell* just happened?" he said, struggling to catch his breath.

It was a shame that such a beautiful man had to be so dim. "Well, a vampire tried to eat you," Ada said. "She was one I was stalking, following a trail of the poor bastards she killed through Europe. I followed both of you on the airship to London, and I just saved your life. You *really* should let me take a look at that. I've dealt with vampire bites before." His eyes were bright, and he was talking and conscious, so maybe the bite wasn't as bad as she originally suspected.

He eyed the stake and mallet in her hands. "Put those down first."

Ada obediently dropped them to the floor, where they landed with muted thumps on the thick carpet. She removed the vial of holy water from her pocket, dampening her handkerchief with it. "Let me take a look," she said again. This next part would hurt like hell, but she didn't want to tell him that. She needed him to trust her, and then... well, she had to figure out a way to keep him from speaking about what he just witnessed, but that could wait until she treated his wound.

He didn't move the shawl away from his neck. "Who are you?"

"Adaline Burgess," she said. "May I take that peek now?"

He gingerly lifted away the shawl, and Ada examined the puncture marks. It wasn't as bad as it looked; Lisette Babineau's lack of thrall meant he fought back hard enough to keep her from ripping out his throat. She pressed her holy water-soaked handkerchief against the wound, wincing at his yelp of pain. "What the hell is that?" he asked again.

"I have to use holy water to clean out a vampire bite," she said. "It'll pass soon, and heal the bite marks. Here, hold this." She pulled his hand up to hold the handkerchief against his neck. "Keep it there until I tell you to let go."

Ada gathered up the greasy clothing lying on the floor and tossed it all in the fire the hotel prepared for Madame Babineau's arrival, followed by the blood-stained shawl. She opened the vampire's valise and was pleased to find a few notes, totalling at least thirty pounds in notes and coins. It was more than enough to tide her over until she could get to a telegraph machine and send an update to the Searchers' New York headquarters.

"Are you stealing Lisette's money?" the man asked incredulously.

"You're worried about my petty theft when she just tried to eat you?" Ada said. "You're unbelievable. We can split it, if you like. Ten pounds."

"I'm not stupid. There was more than that in there."

"Fine, fifteen."

"I don't want any of her money, damn it! I want to know what just happened!" He looked at the fireplace, at the burning pile of clothes. But his gaze remained steady when his eyes met Ada's, and she was assured he wasn't going to swoon or whatever the English did when they were nearly eaten by a vampire. "This didn't just happen."

"It did," Ada said. "Vampires are real, and you just had a very narrow miss with one. I've been tracking her. I do it for a living." She looked back in the valise and removed a pair of kid leather gloves, far nicer than anything she could have afforded. "I'm keeping these, too." She considered it divine payment after her own gloves were ruined by that vampire in Bern. "Are you sure you don't want to split the money she had in here?"

"I have enough money," he said. His eyebrows knit together, and she guessed he wasn't just thinking about Madame Babineau. "I've inherited quite a bit."

Unless he was going to offer her enough for a first class ticket home, she didn't care. Ada slid the gloves into her bag, along with the money. The question of what to do about the man in front of her still loomed in her mind.

But who would believe him when he started babbling about vampires? Ada would hopefully be far away from England by that point and wouldn't have to worry about it. She could go back to hunting vampires on American soil. *So much for my trip to Dresden.*

"Let me take a look at that," she said, lifting the handkerchief off his neck. He cringed but didn't say anything, letting her inspect the damage.

The wound was sealed, the skin already pinkening as it healed. Ada couldn't help but notice the way his pulse fluttered in his throat, full of life and vitality, and she saw why Lisette Babineau was so attracted to this man. He smelled of fresh air and sunshine, the picture of health.

"How is it?" he asked.

"You'll live, and you probably won't even have a scar." She sat down opposite him in a matching chair. "What's your name?"

"Maximilian Sterling."

"*Maximilian*? Really? Do people call you that?"

"Do people call *you* Adaline?" he countered.

"Ada, actually." She looked around the room, taking in the sheer amount of stuff the vampire saw fit to have sent to London. "How long did she rent this room for, Maximilian?"

"It's just Max, and I don't know. I don't know how long she was supposed to be in London. We never got to that part of the conversation."

"Well, we still need to leave." The fire had nearly consumed all of Lisette Babineau's clothing, which pleased Ada. "Do you have somewhere else to stay?"

"I have a flat in Marylebone. I can stay there."

"Let's get you there. Are you all right to walk?"

He stood up and picked up his overcoat, draping it over his arm. His dark eyes caught hers, and despite the possibility that there was more trouble ahead of them, Ada swallowed. He really didn't have the right to be so attractive, and she didn't have the right to notice it. Not when she had vampires to kill.

"I can walk," he said. "But I'm a little dizzy."

"You've lost some blood and you saw me kill a vampire," Ada said. "I'd be more worried if you weren't."

Max was faced with a terrible decision: follow the strange, russet-haired American who just stabbed his would-be lover to death, or stay in the room where her earthly remains were currently being incinerated. He was fairly certain the American wouldn't try to rip out his throat, and she seemed to have an idea of what just happened. He took one last look at the burning clothes in the fireplace.

The American it was.

They slipped out of the room and took the stairs. Halfway down the interminable number of flights, Max's dizziness increased and he had to stop, white-knuckling the banister for balance. He closed his eyes so he wouldn't look down and see how much farther they had to go.

Ada's brow furrowed. "We have to keep moving. There's at least one other vampire in the building."

"Oh, no." Nausea churned in his gut, and he thought he might vomit. "How can you tell?"

"It's a special talent I have," she said, but didn't elaborate further on it. "They might be connected to Lisette Babineau, and if they are, they're going to find that she's really dead now. They'll probably still be able to smell us in that room, so we need to go. Hang on to me if you have to."

Max opened one eye, unable to keep himself from gawking at her. She had to be half a foot shorter than him.

"I'm stronger than I look," she insisted. "Come *on*."

An unearthly squeal from above had them looking up. Something small and dark circled above overhead. A bird? Had a bird taken up residence in one of London's finest hotels?

"*Shit*." Ada paled. "We have to move faster, Max."

"It's just a bird." Max gripped the banister. "Isn't it?"

"It's a bat," she said, hustling down the next flight of stairs. "Or rather, it's a vampire who shifted into its bat form, which means we have to keep moving."

Another screech had Max's head ringing, but he stumbled down the rest of the flight. He let Ada grab his hand, and she pushed a door on to the closest floor, hurrying down the corridor. They stopped at the lift, Ada tossing worried glances over her shoulder.

"You have to get away from here," she said quietly. The lift doors opened, and the operator barely raised an eyebrow when they nearly fell in. "Close the door!" she commanded. The operator gave only the slightest of eye rolls but obeyed.

"I'm putting you in a steam cab," she said.

The lift stopped in the lobby, and Ada grabbed

Max's arm again and led him out of the hotel. The cool night air helped clear his head, and he felt a little of his strength restored, but he didn't shake off Ada's hand. She seemed to know where she was going.

A group of idling cabs waited around the corner, steam issuing from their vents. She led him to one. "Are you going to be all right on your own?" she asked.

"You're leaving me?"

"I have to take care of the rest of that unpleasantness back at the hotel," she said simply. "Before it tracks you down." She didn't add *and bleeds you dry*, but the words hung in the air, unspoken.

"I can't leave you on your own," he said.

"You can and you will." She stepped back, and her eyes raked his form appreciatively. "I'll be honest, Max, I wish I could've spent a little more time with you while in London."

Even though he'd lost a fair amount of blood, Max preened a little at that remark. *A woman after my own heart.* He pulled a slip of paper out of his pocket and wrote down his Euston Road address, and on second thought, his late uncle's estate in Mayfair. *Which is my estate now.*

"I'll be at either of these places," he said. "You're likelier to find me at the first one, though. Are you quite sure you'll be all right?"

She nodded.

It wasn't just that she saved his life tonight. Perhaps it was the way the street lamps shone on her, making her look like some kind of rough-and-tumble angel.

Tumble. Even in his injured state, his mind could still drift in that direction.

Impulsively, he kissed her. She stiffened in surprise for a second, then responded, her arms sliding around his shoulders to bring him nearer to her. She opened her mouth and his tongue eagerly swept inside, drawing a gasp from her.

They were likely inviting attention from passers-by, but he didn't care. The taste of her mouth, the feel of her body through her threadbare coat and heavy dress, was as charged as the electric lamps illuminating the hotel's entrance. There was nothing like a near-death experience to set his blood running high.

She broke it off, pushing him into the waiting cab. The driver looked at them, an amused expression on his face, before flicking away the remains of the cheroot he was smoking. "Ready?" he asked, in a distinctive Cockney drawl.

"Yes." He slid across the battered seat, injecting as much meaning into his next words as he could. "I will be *very* disappointed if you do not call on me during your time here, Ada."

"No monster could stop me," she said. "Have a safe trip, Max." She closed the cab door before the driver could, and he watched her retreating figure walk back to the Langham Hotel.

ADA SLIPPED BACK into the lobby and immediately headed for the first doorway to the stairs she could find. Already she felt a twinge that meant a vampire was close by, and she looked up, half-expecting to see a bat. All she saw were scarred walls and banisters at odds with the elegant decor in the rest of the hotel. She listened, but didn't hear any screams or snarls that indicated a vampire attack was occurring.

Yet.

Stake and mallet in hand, she started up the stairs. *Come out and show yourself, you undead bastard. I have a very important meeting with a fancy-pants Englishman that I'd like to get to as soon as I can.* She was sure she'd even heard his name before, but she quickly shook aside that notion. All English names sounded the same. He probably had far-flung relatives in America who'd helped found major cities or something like that. Still, she didn't entirely discount the idea that she heard the name *Maximilian Sterling* before she arrived in London.

The twinge grew stronger, but when she looked up, she still didn't see a bat. She patted her pocket, feeling the reassuring lump the vial of holy water made, and gripped her stake and mallet a little more tightly as she crept up the stairs.

At the seventh floor, the pulsing behind her eyes told her to stop and take a look around. She was at the end of the corridor, doors lining either side. Frustratingly, she couldn't sense which door the vampire might be hiding behind. *Fool,* she told herself. She should have bribed a clerk downstairs for a list of room numbers and occupants.

She took small, careful steps on the carpet. "I know you know I'm here," she whispered. "Come out and let's get this over with."

A door on the left was wrenched open, about six feet from where she stood. A tall, black-clad vampire, his fangs bared over snarling lips, flew in her direction with lightning speed.

Ada was ready when he lunged at her, and raised her stake in time. Throwing all of her strength behind it, she slammed the mallet into it, landing squarely in the center of his chest.

Surprise bloomed across his pale features.

They're always surprised, she thought, then closed her eyes as he crumbled into greasy ash in front of her. Irritation colored her sense of victory. Now her only good dress for traipsing around England was ruined.

Fucking vampires. She shook ash from her dress and hair as much as she could, and looked at the empty clothes on the floor. The hotel's cleaning staff could puzzle over the pile of ash in the corridor, but the clothing had to go.

Of course he'd been wearing black. The newly turned ones always did.

She paused for half a second, greasy coat in her hands.

If he had just shifted back into his human form from a bat, he would still be naked. There were too many clothes on the floor for him to have dressed in the bare few minutes she saw that bat. Which meant...

A piercing screech sounded far too close to her ear, followed by the flap of wings. "Damn it!" she yelped, forgetting about the human guests on this floor. The huge bat swooped down, grazing her ear, before retreating into the room the dead vampire emerged from.

She tucked her stake and mallet under arm and whipped the holy water from her pocket, uncorking the stopper. She slipped into the room, closing the door behind her.

The room's gas lamps were lit, lending a warm glow to the room. The window was pushed open. Ada's heart sank at the sight. Maybe her quarry already escaped.

The bat whipping across the room, aiming for her head, dispelled her of that notion. She felt wings graze her face, and she closed her eyes, blindly splashing holy water on the awful thing. She heard another shriek of pain that had her ears ringing, and the scent of burning flesh filled her nostrils.

She rubbed holy water out of her own eyes and tossed aside her now-empty vial. She readied her stake and mallet as the bat shifted into a pale, very naked man whose hands kept scrubbing at his burned face. "You bitch!" he snarled. Face still smoking, he jumped at her, knocking her against the walls and forcing all the breath from her lungs.

Ada couldn't be enthralled, and she guessed by the way his eyes bulged and tried to bore into hers that he might have guessed that already. She slipped away from him when he snapped at her, teeth clacking, and ignored the painful throb in her side that meant she'd probably broken a rib again. "What are you doing here?" she asked. "Why are you the third vampire I've come across in the last hour?"

She knew receiving an answer was unlikely, but she still liked to ask.

The vampire surprised her by answering. "Visitors." Then he sniffed the air. "*Dhampir!*"

It wasn't the first time Ada or another Searcher was falsely accused of being a half-human, half-vampire hybrid, although it wasn't too far from the truth. "Not quite," she said. She lunged for the vampire, but only managed to scratch his side. "Shit!" she said. She hated missing her targets.

It still hurt like hell, and he howled, doubling over. Ada raced for him again, stake raised to plunge into his back, but he suddenly snapped to attention, fangs extended.

Oh, fuck. This was going to be bad.

Ice-blue eyes met hers. She moved away, but he

24

grabbed her arm, bony fingers locking into it with an iron grip. Fangs sank into her neck, and she bit back a scream.

She *hated* being bitten, as much as missing a vampire's heart with her stake.

He greedily sucked at the wound he opened, and Ada forced her mind away from the pain. She still held on to her stake and mallet, and with her last ounces of strength she pushed them into the nearest body part she could, hoping the motion would buy her enough time to get away.

The fangs pulled out of her neck. The vampire's lips were still blood-stained as he sputtered and coughed from the pain. He grabbed his ribs, and Ada saw an angry black mark where her stake grazed him. It would leave a scar.

His body crumpled on itself, and for a second Ada thought she might have actually killed him. But as she watched, she saw it wasn't actually crumpling. He shrank, his cold skin turning leathery, wings sprouting from his back. A second later the bat flew out the open window.

"Oh, thank God." She pressed her hand against her neck. Her dress was torn and her fingers came away bloodier than she expected. She was angry about losing the vampire, but he nearly killed her. That had to be the worst attack she'd ever experienced.

She had to get out of here now, before anyone saw her. There wasn't time to clean up the mess in the corridor, or in here. Let the maids faint when they saw the remains, or whatever English maids did when they saw something vile, and the papers publish wild theories. But she knew if anyone saw her with a gaping wound in her neck, with human remains—albeit undead human remains—scattered around her, she wouldn't have a plausible explanation for it. England still hanged murderers.

She frantically looked around the well-appointed room, her gaze landing on a black silk scarf. She wrapped it around her neck, wincing when she touched it and felt blood seeping through the cloth.

This was bad, and she didn't have any holy water to clean the wound, nor did she know of any reliable places in London to ask for more without sounding crazy. Were the nuns here as superstitious as their German counterparts?

She left the room, noting that her vampire sense was no longer going off, although she was increasingly light-headed. She forced herself to take the stairs back to the lobby and avoided eye contact with everyone there until she got outside.

There was still a line of steam cabs waiting outside the Langham Hotel, and she found herself stumbling to the nearest one. *I must have lost more blood than I thought.*

"You all right, miss?" the cab driver asked.

She kept her hand over her scarf, hoping he wouldn't notice the blood smeared around her fingers. "Just fine," she said, but her voice was a croak. With her other hand, she reached into her skirt pocket until she found the piece of paper Max gave her earlier, peering at the address in the dim light offered by the street lamps. Her fingers left bloody smears on the paper. "Can you take me to Euston Road?"

THREE

Max's flat was immaculately clean, just as he left it the last time he was in England nearly a year ago, and he was pleased to see that his landlady kept the place free of dust. He half-stumbled up the stairs well past supper time, hoping Mrs. Boggs didn't notice the wound healing on his neck with remarkable speed.

If she noticed, she didn't let on. "I was expecting you back a few weeks ago," she said. "I was sorry to hear about your uncle." She took his hat and coat, stashing them in a closet, without being prompted, while he surveyed his flat. It was just as he left it the last time he was here, the space tastefully decorated with Mrs. Boggs's touch.

He tilted his head in surprise, winced at the pain, and touched the bite mark. "You heard about that?"

Now it was the landlady's turn to look surprised. "It was all over London when it happened."

For the first time, it shamed Max that he knew so little of his uncle's life, let alone his death. All Silas Weston, the man's long-serving butler, told him in his letters was that it was a "mysterious" death. Uncle James could have drowned. He didn't know how to swim and disliked the water, so it would have been a mystery as to how he would have found himself near water. He could have...

Mrs. Boggs's voice snapped him out of his musing, and he shook his head a little to wake himself up. Lisette had taken far too much blood from him. "It scared a lot of people, of course, but I think a lot of what they wrote about in the papers was rubbish." She continued. "Mr. Weston actually came by here, wanting to know if I knew where in the world you could be. He was very upset."

"Mrs. Boggs, I landed at the Thames Airfield only a few hours ago," he said. "I haven't sent so much as a telegram to Weston, let alone seen him. He wasn't specific in his letters. What happened to my uncle?"

Mrs. Boggs swallowed and briefly looked away. "I shouldn't have said anything. I apologize, Mr. Sterling. I should have waited until you spoke with Mr. Weston." Her gray eyes searched his face. "You *are* going to speak to Mr. Weston? He said you were the older Mr. Sterling's only living relative."

"I'll see him in the morning," Max promised her. "It's been a difficult evening thus far."

"You've been in trouble?"

He nodded. "I was attacked near the Langham Hotel," he said. At her shocked expression, he added, "I'm fine, nothing was taken from me, and the culprit escaped." A lie, but of course he couldn't let her know the truth. "But that's not important. What happened to my uncle?"

Mrs. Boggs paled, and she pushed a strand of graying hair behind her ear. "His body was found in an alley in Wapping," she said. She shook her head. "This isn't my place to tell you. Shall I bring you some supper?"

Wapping? Uneasiness settled over Max.

Food was the farthest thing from his mind, but Max knew he should probably eat something. "Please," he said, then added, "Both to supper, and to telling me what happened to Uncle James."

"It's horrible," she whispered. "I don't believe the stories printed in the papers, but Mr. Weston was quite insistent they were true. Mr. Sterling, your uncle was murdered."

Max deduced as much, as James's body was found in a Wapping alley. There was no reason for the man to be either near an alley or in Wapping. "What happened?" he asked again.

The landlady looked away again, a hand over her mouth. Finally, she said, "Mr. Weston and the papers said he was... exsanguinated. Drained." She gulped. "His blood was gone. Mr. Weston had to identify the body himself, and said he was white as a sheet."

Drained. Max took an involuntary step backward, then touched his neck. "Dear God." It was all he could manage.

He should have brought Ada back to his flat, or stayed with her at the Langham Hotel. Uncle James's death could have been the work of a madman—well, *obviously* it was the work of a madman—but after his experience tonight, there could very well be a supernatural element to it. Lisette Babineau taught him as much, as had that flying vampire bat at the hotel. In an uncharacteristic show of spirituality, Max uttered a quick, silent prayer for his late uncle and for Adaline Burgess's safety.

"Sir?"

The landlady's voice quickly had him offering a mental "amen." "Weston wasn't specific in his letters about my uncle's death," he said. "This is quite a shock. I wish I was informed of it before."

"He said you were traveling and it's so hard to track down travelers," she said. "I'm certain he wouldn't hold that against you."

He might, although the quiet, dignified butler would never say as much. Weston knew the cities Max passed through most often, and Max received three letters over five weeks, in Constantinople, Milan, and Lisbon, all dated the past January, and he ignored all of them. He and James hadn't been close; they hadn't seen each other in over four years. Max could have sent a letter or telegram, or come straight home, and he hadn't.

"He might," Max finally said. "Thank you for telling me, Mrs. Boggs, and I think I would like some supper now."

"I'll heat it up straight away."

"Don't fuss with that," he said. "Cold is fine."

Mrs. Boggs gave him a strange look, but left his flat to put together a tray for him. Whether it was his request for cold food or that he still had an appetite after hearing that his uncle's body was found exsanguinated in a Wapping alleyway, he couldn't tell. Possibly both.

She left him a tray with a generous meal on it for him, and despite the stress of the last few hours, he found he was famished. *It must be the blood loss.* He shoved a piece of chicken in his mouth, savoring Mrs. Boggs's cooking, even if it was cold. It was one of the very few things he missed while abroad.

He unpacked the few belongings he traveled with, taking care to set aside the sheaf of handwritten pages that would later make up his latest adventure novel, to be serialized in whatever magazine might offer him the most money. It was a silly thing, like they all were, loosely based on his own travels, and the hero a highly intelligent dirigible pilot. The fact that the pilot resembled Max was mere coincidence, or so he said when asked.

He finished off the cold beef and considered asking Mrs. Boggs for more, when a knock sounded from the door. "Mr. Sterling?" The landlady's voice was high and frightened.

Max opened the door and a new wave of fear crashed through him at the sight of her pale face. "What's wrong?"

"There's a young lady downstairs asking for you," she said. "She looks unwell, sir." Her voice dropped to a stage whisper. "I think she's American."

Max relaxed, both at her pronouncement and the knowledge that Ada found her way to his flat. "Americans aren't unwell, that's just how they are." He closed the door behind him and followed Mrs. Boggs downstairs.

"She's outside, sir," she said quietly.

Irritation overtook Max as he flung open the front door. Mrs. Boggs had never been hospitable to foreigners. His irritation immediately gave way to concern when he saw a bedraggled dress and Ada's pale, drawn face in the light thrown off by the streetlamps. She held a dark scarf against her neck, but Max could still see the blood drying on her hand.

She tried to smile. "Surprise."

"Oh my God." Max gathered her in his arms and pulled her inside. She swayed on her feet in the foyer, never letting go of the scarf. "Mrs. Boggs, can you get some water and bandages?" He motioned to pick up Ada, but she shook her head.

"I just need to sit down," she said, her voice hoarse and scratchy. "I can walk just fine." Still, she let him lead her upstairs to his flat and draped herself across his settee.

"What the hell happened?"

Instead of answering his question, she asked, "You wouldn't happen to have any holy water around, would you? I used up mine back at the hotel."

"I don't. I'm not a religious man, I'm afraid."

She winced. "God damn it. Is there a church near here? They're pretty generous with the holy water in New York."

"I'll ask Mrs. Boggs, or I can fetch some. St. Pancras isn't too far from here."

"I haven't lost too much blood, I think, but it hurts like a son of a bitch and it'll keep hurting until I can clean the bite with holy water. I can go if you give me directions." She shifted her head against the settee cushions and cringed.

Max sidestepped her comment about going back out into the night. "You were bitten?"

"Yes, but you should see the other guys." She tried to smile and failed. "Well, one of them. He's a pile of ash back at the hotel. I just need to keep pressure on this until I can get to some holy water." She sat up and winced again. "Just tell me where this church is and I'll go. Are there any nuns there? They're usually very nice."

"St. Pancras isn't Catholic, and you will do nothing of the sort," Max said firmly. He pulled on his coat and hat, then paused. "Does it have to be a Catholic church?"

"They're usually the ones with holy water."

"The Church of England still observes Communion." He slid on his gloves. "All Henry the Eighth wanted was a divorce, after all."

"As long as it's blessed, it should work."

Mrs. Boggs appeared in the doorway, bearing a pitcher of warm water and some bandages. "Where are you going?" she said to Max.

"I have to fetch some medicine our guest needs," he said briskly. "I won't be gone long." Remembering his manners, he added, "Mrs. Boggs, this is my friend, Adaline Burgess of America. Ada, this is Mrs. Boggs, my landlady." He turned to leave the flat, then remembered one more thing. "Ada, does this medicine cost anything?"

Ada sighed, but there was a slight smile on her face, despite what had to be incredible pain coursing through her. "It's polite to offer a donation."

THE TALL WHITE columns of St. Pancras Church nearly glowed in the light offered by nearby streetlamps, giving it an air of safety and refuge. Never being a religious man, nor one with a particular interest in architecture, Max had never taken notice of the church in all his years flitting in and out of his rented flat. It was a beautiful building, he decided. He hoped whoever he found inside would have a kind spirit to match, one who didn't ask too many questions.

He paused in front of the great doors, unsure how to word his request for help. Ada had said clergy would be only too happy to give away a small amount of holy water in exchange for a few coins. She had been talking about her experiences with Catholic churches. Would their Anglican counterparts be so generous?

Stop dallying. Ada is suffering from vampire bites in your flat because of you. Go inside, ask for holy water, and if there is no one to ask, help yourself.

Max took a deep breath and pulled at one of the doors. It opened easily on well-oiled hinges. He stepped inside, blinking as his vision adjusted to the interior illumination. To his surprise, gas lamps gave off a pleasant yellow light, highlighting the richly colored carpet that muffled his footsteps. There was a faint scent of cleaning products in the air, a fragrance at odds with the quiet luxury of the church's vestibule. A wooden rack of handbills and pamphlets stood a few feet away.

He took a few careful steps out of the vestibule into the nave. The pews were empty. At the opposite end of the massive room was a pulpit, its polished wood shining under the light offered by gas lamps turned to low. Behind it, organ pipes stretched to the ceiling, causing Max to temporarily wonder where the rest of the instrument was hidden.

"May I help you?"

The voice was male, quiet, and made Max nearly jump out of his skin. He whirled around to see a slender, fair-haired man behind him. He looked young at first, perhaps in his early twenties, but when Max looked closer, he saw lines of tension bracketing his eyes and mouth. The white clerical collar around his neck was a sharp contrast to his black shirt, over which he wore an obviously handmade brown wool cardigan.

It took a few second for Max to find his voice. "Good evening, Reverend." He cleared his throat. "I have an odd request."

The clergyman stiffened. "Oh?"

"Is it possible to procure some holy water from you? I don't need much."

The reverend visibly relaxed. Max wondered what the hell he'd been asked for in the past to warrant such apprehension. As far as bizarre requests went, one for holy water had to be minor. "I see," the reverend replied. "I can arrange that. Will you be requiring the services of the clergy, as well?"

"I don't think so, just the water. I can pay you for it."

"I don't accept payment for it, although the church would appreciate a small donation for its works in the community, if that won't be a hardship to you. Follow me." The reverend strode away in the same direction Max had come from. "Are you Catholic?" he asked over his shoulder.

Max didn't detect a trace of judgement in his tone, although he still hesitated over his answer.

"No, I was actually baptized Anglican, but I'm not a churchgoer."

The reverend's reply was wry. "No matter. We often call it font water in this particular flavor of Christianity."

Max would have felt like an idiot over that error, had he had time for research. He thought about Ada and hoped she wasn't suffering too greatly in his delays.

The reverend opened a cabinet in the vestibule that had escaped Max's notice when he entered. He pressed a small stoppered bottle into Max's hands, the glass cool against his skin. "Are you certain you won't have need of the clergy for this task?"

"I am, but thank you for the offer."

The reverend scrutinized Max's features in the lamps' yellow light. He tried not to look away under the intensity of his gaze. "Whatever you are battling, I pray you are successful," the reverend finally said.

This close to the man, Max could better see his features. The worry lines around his eyes and mouth were misleading; he was definitely as young as he'd initially thought. The reverend's expression was earnest, full of concern. Of course, he would be familiar with evil in the world. Max wondered if he knew about the existence of vampires and their waves of destruction across the world. "Thank you," he finally replied. "I would greatly appreciate that." He remembered his manners and removed a few coins from his pocket, handing them to the reverend.

The other man stared at the shillings in his palm. "This is far too much."

"I won't hear of that. You've done a great service to me tonight." Max thought about Ada, how he had to return to her as soon as possible. "Thank you, Reverend."

The clergyman nodded. "May the Lord protect you."

~

ALL ADA COULD DO WAS hope Max didn't come across any vampires while he was out, and that English vicars were as generous with holy water as American nuns. She wasn't completely incapacitated and she wasn't dying; the bite hurt and the pain was spreading. That son of a bitch hadn't intended to drain her, only rip open something important and let her bleed to death instead. His

message had been clear: "You aren't fit to eat."
The wound throbbed under her hand.

"May I clean that for you?" The landlady eyed
her suspiciously and gestured to Ada's neck.

"No, thank you." Ada forced herself to sit up.
"It's just a scratch." At Mrs. Boggs's look of disbe-
lief, she added, "Wounds around the head and
neck often look worse than they are." Which could
be true, when the cause of the bite wasn't a vampire. "I'll need what Max is picking up for me to
really clean this out."

"What happened, if you don't mind my
asking?"

"Attack," she said. "Outside the Langham
Hotel."

"My word! Something similar happened to Mr.
Sterling tonight, too! We should inform the constables!"

Ada shook her head, wincing at the pain. "No.
No police, Mrs. Boggs."

"You were assaulted! Between Mr. Sterling's
uncle being drained of blood and those other mur-
ders around London, I—"

Ada cut her off. "Drained? What the hell are
you talking about?"

Mrs. Boggs faltered. "You should speak to Mr.
Sterling about that."

"You're telling me Max's uncle was drained?"
Despite her pain, Ada needed to know as much as
she could about a possible vampire infestation in
London. Forget that—there *was* a vampire infestation in London. There were vampire infestations in
every major city, it seemed, but the question was
how bad it was.

The woman's lips remained pinched shut, but
there was a worried look in her pale eyes, so Ada

tried another tack. "Please, Mrs. Boggs, I'm not trying to be nosy. I just… there were similar attacks in New York recently."

The landlady sniffed at that.

Are people here born with sticks up their asses, or do they get them in finishing school? Did landladies go to finishing school? Ada had never been especially interested in the English class system.

"Fine, don't tell me anything. But could you get me another bandage? This one's full." Even through her pain, a small smile tugged at her mouth at the look of disgust on Mrs. Boggs's face. But the landlady obliged.

"You wouldn't happen to have some whiskey around here?" It wouldn't get rid of the pain, but it would make it more bearable.

That warranted another sniff from the landlady. "I do not keep spirits in my house," she said stiffly. "You will have to ask Mr. Sterling when he returns. He may have a bottle somewhere."

If Ada wasn't so weak, she would have poked around the flat herself, but she was, so she stayed put on the couch. How far away was that church, anyway? She hoped Max was okay.

She hadn't lost enough blood that she was in danger of passing out, but she was tired and her body confused about the time since she arrived in Europe. Now it was catching up with her, and she had to fight to keep her eyes open. *Do not fall asleep. It will be very bad if you fall asleep before Max gets back with the holy water.* She might not wake up for a couple of days if she slept now.

She bunched the scarf against her neck and forced herself to stand up. Her head protested, but she soon felt steadier, a little more awake. There was an overstuffed bookcase against the opposite wall, a worn wicker basket carelessly shoved against it. The basket overflowed with magazines and the books were well-read, their spines cracked. The sight was unusual in the otherwise immaculately kept room.

Reading would keep her awake until Max returned with the holy water. She spied copies of *Murray's Magazine* and *The Union Jack* in the basket. "Do you think Max will mind if I read these?" she asked, not caring what Mrs. Boggs's answer might be.

The landlady regarded her coolly. "Probably not."

"Just trying to be polite." Now that it was clear Ada wasn't dying, Mrs. Boggs didn't seem to care as much about her guest. "I guess it could go either way." Though she was pretty sure Max wouldn't care if she read one of his magazines. She'd saved his life tonight, after all.

Crossing the room, she pawed through the pile of newsprint, cringing at the bloody smear she left across one. "Max doesn't strike me as the periodical sort," she mused aloud.

Mrs. Boggs let out a barely perceptible sigh, but the noise still set Ada's teeth on edge. Why was she so determined to be unpleasant? "Mr. Sterling writes for some of them," she said dismissively. "Adventure stories or some such nonsense. I don't have the time to read them, myself."

Ada picked up *Murray's Magazine*, a publication she could only occasionally get her hands on in New York, and thumbed through the newsprint until she stopped at a dog-eared page. "'The Same Old Sea Over the Ocean,'" she read aloud. "By Maximilian Sterling." She noted the illustration of the elaborate dirigible, and remembered where she heard Max's name before. "I've read his stories!" she said excitedly. "That's who he is!"

Another sigh came from Mrs. Boggs. "You're surprised I can read?" she said over her shoulder. She pulled out another magazine and brought both of them back to the couch with her.

"Yes." At least the landlady was honest.

"I'm not an expert on the English language, but I'm literate," Ada said. She lay back against the couch's stiff cushions, not caring that her ankles and much-mended stockings were visible, and began to read, trying to take her mind off her wound. She loved the British magazines, and they were so hard to come by in America. She liked what she read of Max's Captain Reed series, the stories about the dirigible captain who traveled and gambled his way across the world.

"Does he know Doyle?" she asked Mrs. Boggs. "He lives in London, doesn't he?"

"I wouldn't know his acquaintances. Mr. Sterling is rarely here."

"He wrote *A Study in Scarlet*. My brother gave me *Beeton's Christmas Annual* last year."

That earned yet another disdainful look from the landlady. "I do not indulge in such frivolity, Miss Burgess."

Footsteps sounded on the stairs leading to the flat, and Ada smiled. She sat up and shook her skirts over her legs, lest Mrs. Boggs insist on continuing to be scandalized, and set aside the magazine. Now she had another task besides vampire hunting before her: buy more magazines to take home. Her brothers would appreciate them, too. The door opened and Max stepped in, slightly out of breath. "You're all right?" he asked by way of greeting.

Ada nodded and set aside the magazines. "I

am, aside from the neck wound. You never told me you're Maximilian Sterling, adventure author."

"It didn't occur to me when I was being assaulted." He withdrew a bag from his coat pocket and set it on the table in front of her.

"Will you be requiring my assistance, sir?" Mrs. Boggs asked.

Max shot a quizzical look at Ada. She replied for him. "No."

"That will be all," Max said firmly.

"If you require anything, please let me know," Mrs. Boggs said, but the offer sounded hollow.

As soon as the door closed, Ada said, "She's terribly pleasant, isn't she?"

"Delightful. You didn't have any problems while I was away?"

She shook her head. "Vampires can't come into a home occupied by humans uninvited. You have some holy water?"

He removed a glass bottle from his coat pocket, a larger vessel than she had been expecting. "The reverend insisted that my donation was too much."

"So is all that holy water. But before you start, you wouldn't happen to have a bottle of whiskey around here, would you? This" —she pointed to the bottle— "is going to hurt like hell, as you know."

Max disappeared into the kitchen and she heard him poking through a cabinet before reappearing with a bottle. "This is Scottish and it's potent." He poured measures into two glasses and set them on the table. "Will that do?"

Ada didn't wait for him to make a toast or whatever silly thing men did when they saw a woman drinking hard liquor. She splashed it back in one gulp and relished the harsh burn coursing down her throat. "All right," she said. "Let's get this over with."

Max took a delicate sip from his glass and made a face. "I would've figured you were a whiskey man," she said wryly as he uncorked the milk bottle. He splashed some of the holy water on the clean rags Mrs. Boggs left them.

"I like it well enough." He held up the rag and Ada tilted her head to the side, removing her scarf from the wound.

She saw him blanch. "That bad?"

"It's— Your skin is turning gray at the site."

"Vampire bites will do that. Just hold that against my neck until I stop screaming."

Max's eyes widened, but he obliged.

Her vision swam and the burning pain was intense enough to make her breath catch, but Ada didn't scream, only moaned. She clenched her jaw shut against the searing pain and dug her nails into the couch cushions. She forced herself to breathe through her nose and finally managed to say, "Little more."

"Are you certain?"

"Yes, I'm fucking certain! It's a vampire bite, Max. It has to be cleaned before I get an infection!"

Max did so, and this time the burning wasn't as bad. "I'm not trying to be rude," she said. "But it's been a couple of hours since I was bitten and I really should to get back out there." The pain was already starting to fade. She lifted the rag and felt the mark. It would probably leave a scar; she hadn't had the holy water on it quickly enough.

"You should rest," Max said.

"I said I *should* go, not that I will. A recovering vampire hunter should wait to regain her strength first, even if they want to go out and finish the job." She wasn't stupid enough to go out following this kind of attack. She needed sleep.

"You're welcome to stay here," he offered.

Despite the circumstances, Ada's interest was piqued. Again. She'd been interested since she saw him boarding the dirigible with Lisette Babineau. And even though she had that windfall burning a hole in her pocket since she'd staked the French vampire, she was still perilously short on funds. A free place to sleep was an unexpected perk.

Except… "In your bed?"

He raised an eyebrow, eyes twinkling despite the gravity of their situation. "Yes. Although I won't be there."

She was disappointed to hear that. "Because you're a gentleman?"

His voice took on a timbre that sent a bolt of heat straight through her. "No, because a vampire tried to tear out your throat. When we share a bed, I want you to have as much energy as possible. You'll need it."

FOUR

Max slept fitfully on his settee. It was too short for his legs, but he wasn't about to complain. He woke up with the dawn, a crick in his neck and his knees stiff, discomforts he walked off before checking in on his guest.

Ada was wrapped up in the bedcovers, only the top of her head with its messy, russet-colored curls visible. She stirred a little and he left, closing the bedchamber door behind him. He was a little disappointed that she wasn't awake yet.

He had been avoiding the pile of newspapers Mrs. Boggs left for him, but with nothing to do until Ada woke up, he finally opened one broadsheet. His uncle's murder was splashed across the pages, as the discovery of the drained body of one of London's finest medical authorities was wont to encourage. Max felt his stomach turn over as he took in the details, all written in gleeful, gory detail. James Sterling was found bloodless, whiter than the paper the news was printed on, with puncture marks on his throat according to one of the morgue workers the reporter had spoken to.

Max set aside the paper and pressed his palms

against his eyes. Tears welled up there and he brushed them away impatiently. He'd been an utter cad, stomping around Europe and writing his adventure stories, burning through the inheritance his late parents left him, and ignoring all letters and wires from home. He'd thought Silas Weston was exaggerating the strangeness of Uncle James's death to lure him home to a country he'd never liked, all in an attempt to turn him into someone he wasn't: respectable, docile, proper.

There had been no one to mourn James Sterling the man, just the eccentric doctor whose obsessive research into blood made him an oddity among London's physicians. Max had been embarrassed by the man in life, and for the first time he felt ashamed for that. James had put him through school, paid for his university education. And what had Max done to repay him? *I took off for parts unknown as soon as I reached my majority, with my parents' money, to write silly stories.*

And then he'd been eaten by a vampire. After what Max saw last night, of that there was no doubt. And the St. Pancras reverend who had given him the holy water hadn't seemed terribly surprised by Max's request; he'd even seemed used to being asked for it.

Max picked up the broadsheets again, this time scanning through the print for something about other strange deaths. He found a few lines in two papers that detailed drained bodies of vagrants, one in Whitechapel, the other in Wapping. The latter was found near where James's body was discovered. All had puncture marks on their throats, but they were too small and precise to be made by human teeth according to a constable quoted in the paper. A madman was loose on London streets, the constable was quoted as saying, but he certainly wasn't a vampire, because vampires weren't real.

He had to pay a visit to James's Mayfair home as soon as possible. Silas Weston must know something the papers hadn't reported. The butler had been fiercely loyal to his employer since Max was a child. There had to be a clue somewhere in the house that the police overlooked or outright ignored.

Max quickly washed and dressed. Then he called Mrs. Boggs for some breakfast to be brought up. The landlady presented him with a tray bearing a teapot and scones, nothing else. "I haven't been to market yet," she said by way of excusing the meager meal, but the pointed look she threw at the closed bedroom door told Max she disapproved of his overnight guest.

The door opened and Ada crept out, a hand over her yawning mouth, as soon as Mrs. Boggs left the flat. "She makes me look like one of those irritating morning people," she said by way of greeting.

"Did you sleep well?" He handed her a cup of steaming tea.

She wore Max's robe over whatever she'd worn to bed last night. Her shift, probably, an image he liked very much. "As well as I could expect, given the gaping vampire bite in my neck. How's yours, by the way?" She thumped heavily into the settee, cup in hand. She took a sip and made a face, but didn't comment on it. Perhaps she preferred coffee.

"I think it's going to be fine." He hadn't even thought about the bite since he woke up. He reached out and touched the wound, feeling smooth skin. "You arrived just in time."

"I saved you *and* your pretty neck." She cast

him an appreciative look over the rim of her cup, sending a wave of heat through his body. Damn it, but she could be so distracting when he should be concentrating on what caused their bites and Uncle James's death.

"What about yours?" he asked.

She still had a scarf loosely wrapped around her neck, and she unwound it and tilted her head to the side, baring her skin for his inspection. "How bad is it?"

It looked worse than his felt. It was vastly improved from last night, but the skin was still pink and raw, and now Max could see teeth impressions still healing on her skin. Tellingly, there were puncture marks too small and round to be made by human teeth, just like the rags wrote about his uncle's body. As alluring as he found Ada to be, he couldn't suppress a shudder.

Ada turned away, a petulant look crossing her face. "I guess it's still bad."

"No!" Max quickly protested. He gulped down a mouthful of weak tea. "It's not that. I understand why the vampire wanted to bite you."

Ada managed an eye roll at that. "He was angry and hungry?"

"It also looks edible. Believe me, if I found myself of the bloodsucking persuasion, yours is exactly the kind of neck I'd seek out."

She blushed. "Max, please. We've already saved each other's bacon and we met about…" She checked the grandfather clock against the wall. "Maybe twelve hours ago?" She turned surprised eyes to him. "Good God, is it really a quarter past seven?"

Max picked up the broadsheets and held them out to her. "It's not you or the bite, Ada. It's these."

47

She tentatively accepted them and scanned the headlines, eyes widening as she read through the columns detailing James's gruesome murder.

Max refilled his teacup as Ada flipped through the papers. Finally, she set them aside. "Max, I'm so sorry," she said softly.

Part of him didn't want her sympathy, but he couldn't help but feel grateful for it, that he wasn't alone in this nightmare. He hoped she might know what to do next, because he sure as hell didn't. "There's no need for it."

When he looked back at her, her eyes were oddly shiny. For the first time, it occurred to him that she very likely knew people who had been killed by vampires. "But it's what you say when your friend's uncle has been murdered, isn't it? And I'd say we're friends, even if we didn't know each other yesterday afternoon."

"Vampire attacks have that effect on people, don't they?" Despite his flip words, Max couldn't shake off the guilty feelings over not returning to England as soon as he received Silas Weston's first letter.

"They do." She looked away and wiped her eye. She took a final sip of tea before standing up. "I assume you want to visit your uncle's house today?"

He nodded. "As quickly as possible. Will you accompany me?"

"Of course. I just have to get dressed." She made for the bedroom, then paused. "Is there anywhere near here where I can send a cable?"

≈

AFTER QUICKLY DRESSING in Max's bedroom, Ada counted out her bounty: thirty-seven pounds in British sterling and one hundred French francs. It was certainly enough to replenish her meager funds until she went home. She couldn't remember the last time she had so much money.

She forced her curly hair into one of the respectable, uncomfortable buns Englishwomen were so fond of, wincing at the ache the pins left in her scalp. It was high time women should be allowed to wear their hair loose or at least comfortably in England. No one cared one whit what her hair looked like back in New York. But her clothing already spoke of a poor background, and she didn't want to embarrass Max any further by not making at least a token effort to blend in while in England. She wiped off the ash stains from the fights at the hotel last night as best she could. At least her dress was dark blue, making them less obvious.

She checked her reflection in the looking glass, sighed at the sight of the healing bite mark, and tugged her collar as high as she could in a vain effort to conceal it. Finally, she wrapped a scarf around her neck. It was far too matronly for Ada's tastes, but it would have to do.

She stuck a scone in her mouth when she and Max left the flat, where they met a disapproving Mrs. Boggs at the foot of the stairs. *Damn it.* Of all the times she could run into the woman again, of course it would be when she was chewing on a dry scone.

Well, you're not staying here permanently, thank God. After today you won't be seeing much of her.

She swallowed her bite of scone and wrapped the rest in a dingy but clean handkerchief she pulled from her pocket. "Good morning," she said brightly. "Thank you for the tea."

Mrs. Boggs regarded her coolly. For a few seconds, Ada thought she might ignore her completely, but the landlady's manners wouldn't let her. "It was my pleasure," she replied stiffly. To Max, she said, "You are aware, Mr. Sterling, that your agreement with me states you are the only person who may live in those rooms?"

"I'm well aware of that, Mrs. Boggs, but I thank you for the reminder." Without waiting for a reply, Max opened the door, ushering Ada through.

"I apologize for that," he said as soon as they were in the street.

"No need for it."

"I've had other companions spend the night with me before, and she's never…" He must have realized what he was saying, but Ada brushed it off.

"I don't care about your mistresses, Max," she said.

"They weren't *all* mistresses…"

"You don't owe me an explanation. I'm a crude American, and even I think that was unspeakably rude." He walked briskly, and she was able to keep up. Thank God she could get away with wearing low-heeled boots and still be sort of fashionable.

Max stopped abruptly, earning irritated looks from passersby. "I don't think you're crude," he said, his voice unusually serious.

"Max, it doesn't hurt my feelings. I know there's a big cultural difference between us, and…"

He cut her off. "I like that you're outspoken and bold. Very much so. They're traits women aren't often encouraged to develop." He straightened. "I've also been unspeakably rude to you, as well." He held out his arm.

"That isn't necessary." It was a token protest, but Ada still linked her hand through his.

"It is. I'm pleased to be seen with you, and I am more than happy to escort you to a telegraph office before we make our way to Uncle James's home."

The telegraph office turned out to be located just a few streets from Max's flat, and it was newly opened and surprisingly busy for such an early hour. The office was larger than Ada expected, with six people just to send cables, and a booth that sold dirigible tickets. A hand-painted sign by the ticket booth proclaimed reduced prices on return trip fares anywhere in Britain. Against one wall a floor-to-ceiling shelf rested, bearing souvenirs and books for sale.

Ada picked up a telegram slip and quickly filled it out, noting the outrageous per-letter price list posted on the wall as she did so. Her pencil hovered over the slip, unsure. Should she stick to the Searchers' preferred code names, thereby possibly drawing attention to herself, or spend the extra money and use full words? She didn't know this country, and she didn't know how a cable that was obviously in code would be received at a proper London telegraph office. No one in New York would care what her cables said, only that she paid for them. Finally, she quickly scribbled her message and hoped no one asked any questions, leaving Max's uncle's Mayfair address for the Searchers to use to contact her.

She took a spot in the shortest line, and in less time than she expected, faced the clerk. She pushed her cable message across the desk separating them, and he eyed it warily, his eyes flickering back and forth over the few words written there. Nervousness lodged in the pit of her stomach, a hard ball that she was unaccustomed to.

"Miss, you've misspelled 'they're,'" he finally said.

That was what made him look so concerned? That she was a poor speller? Ada nearly laughed with relief. "Excuse me?"

Hearing her accent, the clerk offered her a condescending smile and turned around the slip. "You wrote 'there here in London' when you meant '*they're* here in London.' I can fix that for you if you like."

Damn, she could never remember the difference between those words. "Send it as is," she said. "The extra letter cost is a little expensive, don't you think?"

The clerk gave a very ungentlemanly-like snort at that. "Words of wisdom."

After she paid for the cable and spied Max looking at the cheap wooden toys lining the shelves, she realized she hadn't yet told Max what she was. Not just the Searcher part, but why she qualified as one in the first place.

This was going to be an awkward conversation, and one they needed to have soon. She had a feeling he might not be totally revolted by her revelation, but she reminded herself that they hadn't known each other a full day prior. She knew nothing about him, save that she enjoyed his writing and he was very far above her in terms of class and station. So far, all they had in common were vampire attacks and physical attraction. He might not share the latter with her after she told him about the Searchers, and that would be a deep shame. The man was breathtaking.

She thought it might be best to tell him as soon

as they arrived at his uncle's house. Max seemed to be a reasonable man. Obviously there hadn't been any time last night to tell him about her particular talent and how she came to inherit it. He might not be so amenable to a proverbial romp in the hay with her after she told him, but she was fairly certain he would still want her help in solving his uncle's murder.

"I've sent my cable. Are you ready to leave?" she asked.

He nearly dropped the carved wooden horse he held.

"Bit jumpy, are we?" she asked.

"More than a bit." He had the faintest of dark circles under his eyes, undoubtedly a result of his blood loss and poor sleep the night before, which made Ada realize she probably looked like utter hell. Between her clothing, accent, curly hair that she could already feel escaping from its uncomfortable knot, and her own vampire bite, she was surprised she hadn't sent anyone crossing the street after they laid eyes on her.

"Do you collect wooden animals?" she asked.

He blinked at her, then looked at the horse in his hand. He quickly set it back on the shelf. "No. It was either look at toys or buy a dirigible ticket." He pointed to the ticket counter. More to himself, he added, "I am not running away from this."

"I'm pleased to hear that, because I wouldn't know the first place to look for your uncle's house."

"Mayfair."

"I have no idea where Mayfair is."

"We'll hire a cab," he said.

Once outside, he hailed a steam cab, much like the ones lined up outside the Langham Hotel last night, but dingier. Ada spotted a few rust spots and scorch marks on the vehicle's roof that she couldn't guess at. Steam-powered cabs were still a rare novelty in New York, and she hadn't taken one until she landed in Berlin. The interior of this cab smelled strongly of tobacco and spilled gin, but Max seemed unfazed by the odor. Ada didn't mention it, as she had smelled much worse in her life. It was dirty, but not unsafe.

"You were able to send your cable without incident?" Max asked.

Ada nodded. "The clerk corrected me on my spelling."

Now, why on earth had she told him that? Max had mentioned attending university and she knew he wrote for a living. Ada left school when she was thirteen and had been slaughtering monsters since then. Once again, she was painfully aware of the gap in their social stations.

"Your spelling?" He turned to her incredulously. "That's impolite."

Ada let out a breath she hadn't known she was holding. "I just told him I didn't want to pay extra for the 'e' in 'you're.'"

Max laughed. "That's a common error, and a dignified way of covering it up." His eyes darted to the driver, who didn't appear to notice his customers as he guided the cab through London's crowded streets. "You mentioned a group you work for before."

"There's a London branch, but I'm not sure how to get there yet." The Searchers were deliberately vague about their headquarters around the world, divulging addresses only when necessary even to members. It was a security issue. She would receive a reply and a meeting place when the New York office read her cable and informed London she was there for an extended visit, but that would be at least a day or two away.

She stole a look at Max. With time and training, maybe he could be a fine vampire slayer, but they didn't have that right now.

The scenery changed when they rode into Mayfair, and Ada had to force herself not to let her jaw drop at the opulence passing them by. The homes here were massive affairs that undoubtedly held only a respectably small family and an army of servants. The gardens and the streets themselves were immaculately clean. Even the sky was a clearer blue here than it had been near Max's Marylebone flat, and Ada found that to be a lovely area as well. Certainly nicer than the narrow house she shared with her brothers and a sister-in-law back in Brooklyn. She had read about clean, sterile streets as these, in Max's stories in fact, but never thought they really existed outside of the pages of a novel or periodical.

She was out of her element. She was more uncomfortable here than she had ever been facing a vampire, stake in hand. These little castles weren't supposed to exist outside of fairy tales.

Neither should vampires, she reminded herself.

The driver let them out in front of an imposing brick home, the shades pulled over all the windows. Ada looked up at all three stories and couldn't suppress a shiver, nor a small nudge of indignation. The house looked large enough to contain the entire row of townhouses her home was in the middle of, and as far as she knew, only Max's uncle had lived in there.

And now it was Max's. She saw by the set of his shoulders as he walked briskly to the front door that he didn't seem terribly thrilled about the prospect.

He opened the door himself and held it for Ada. The foyer was brightly lit, with electric sconces lining the walls. The carpet under their feet was a deep blood-red, and so thick it muffled their footsteps. The furniture was dark wood, heavy and uncomfortable-looking. It felt more like a mausoleum than a home. Immediately, Ada could see why Max didn't like coming back here. The house was too cold for someone as warm as he was.

"Sir?"

The voice sounded from a corridor off the foyer, and the shuffle of feet whispered over the carpet. An older, silver-haired man quickly hastened his pace when he saw Max.

"Hello, Weston," Max said wearily.

"Let me take your coat, sir."

"That's not necessary."

"I'm very pleased to see you," the old man said. "Please allow me to reiterate my deepest condolences on the loss of your uncle."

"James's passing is why I'm here, Weston, and I apologize for not arriving sooner." Max straightened, his coat over his arm. Weston's hand gripped the garment, and Max finally relinquished it. "Weston, this is Adaline Burgess, a friend of mine from America. I'll need a room prepared for her."

"Of course, sir." Weston turned to face her, an expectant look on his weathered face.

Oh, hell. Ada knew her manners were lacking, but until now she didn't know just how badly. She bent her knees, starting to curtsey, but a cough from Max had her straightening up. "Your coat," Max murmured.

Oh, that. Ada exhaled and pasted a smile on her face. She let Weston help her out of her coat, and he accepted her satchel without a word on its shabby condition. "Thank you." Was she supposed to thank servants? She would in New York, if she'd known anyone with a butler. It just seemed the polite thing to do.

If she made a faux pas, Weston didn't let on. "Your rooms are ready, sir," he said. "I've been expecting you. I can have some dinner prepared, if you like."

"I'm not hungry, but tea would be appreciated. Ada?" Max turned to her.

The scone she'd wolfed down earlier in the morning was a long-ago memory. It was a bit early for a midday meal, but as long as Weston was offering… "I would like something to eat, please," she said.

Weston nodded. "Very good. I will prepare a tray for you."

He put away their coats and led them up a curving, carpeted staircase. The balustrade, like everything else in the house, was dark wood, so highly polished Ada didn't want to touch it and leave fingerprints behind. A small landing separated a pair of staircases leading to separate wings, and they turned left.

Hm. Maybe she and Max would have rooms close to each other. If he was still amenable to a romp, that would prove convenient.

"Will the blue room be sufficient for your guest?" Weston asked.

"The blue room is fine, Weston, thank you." Max opened the first door they passed and looked inside. This must be his space.

The butler opened the door to a room next

door and gestured inside. "Will this be suitable, Miss Burgess?" he asked.

She didn't detect a hint of condescension in the butler's voice. Maybe the citizens of Mayfair weren't as snobby as she'd been expecting.

She stepped into a beautifully appointed room that reminded her of the luxury of the Langham Hotel's rooms before she sprayed them with dead vampires. A four-poster bed rested in the middle of the room, flanked by heavy nightstands on either side. The bedding was embroidered with twisting gold thread, covering a thick mattress and pillows. Weston opened the drapes, letting in morning sunshine and revealing the gold-flocked deep green wallpaper.

"This is perfect," she pronounced. "Thank you, Mr. Weston."

"Just Weston," he gently corrected her.

"Weston, then."

"I shall have that tray fixed for you, Miss Burgess."

She thought about asking him to call her Ada, but had a feeling he wouldn't. Instead, she nodded. "Much appreciated."

"Weston," Max called from his bedchamber, "Have that tray put together in the dining room, and make yourself available. We need to speak with you."

A murmur of acknowledgement and the sound of footsteps over the carpet told her Weston was complying. Ada unwrapped the scarf from her neck and touched her healing wound. She then checked it in the large looking glass positioned against the wall. It was healing nicely, and she decided to leave the scarf off. Dark circles ringed her eyes, but there was nothing she could do about those.

She unpinned her hair and closed her eyes. As she massaged feeling back into her scalp, she couldn't keep a moan of pleasure from escaping her.

"That's the happiest I've ever seen you look." Max's voice was low in her ear, full of suggestion.

Ada turned around. "I can't believe I didn't hear you." What kind of vampire hunter was she if she didn't hear her quarry around her?

"I'm good at being stealthy."

"Will I scandalize your butler if I go down for lunch with my hair undone?"

"He's too professional and used to the eccentric ways of the Sterling family to say anything."

"So you often left your rooms with your hair unbound?" she teased.

"Always."

The look in his eyes sent a wave of heat through her body, and she leaned forward. Her belly quivered in anticipation, remembering the kiss they shared at the hotel last night, and how it wasn't nearly enough for her.

His mouth found hers, teasing her lips open. Her breath stuttered as she responded, hands curling around his shoulders. They were just as firm as she suspected them to be.

His hand found her hair, fingers running through it. "This is lovely and it's a shame you keep it tied away," he murmured against her mouth.

Her stomach growled, ruining the moment. She pulled away reluctantly. "Um," she said.

"Blood loss will make you hungry," he replied sagely.

His words reminded her that she still hadn't told him about why she was a Searcher, and she needed to do that, as soon as possible. "Max," she said, but he had already taken her arm and was leading her out of the room, down the corridor.

"Yes?"

His voice still held the lazy trace of lust it took on when he looked at her, and she hated that she might be putting a damper on those feelings. "I need to tell you something," she said urgently. "I should have before, but, you know … vampires."

"Is it about the vampires?"

"Sort of. And me," she added.

They descended the stairs, and Ada could picture dukes and duchesses doing the same thing, on the same stairs, before adoring crowds of well-heeled friends. "Are you a vampire?" he asked lightly, but she detected the wariness in his voice.

"No."

"You have an uncanny ability to detect them," he said.

So, he noticed that. Maybe her confession wouldn't terrify him. "I'm human," she assured him. "But not all of my ancestors were."

He didn't push her arm away, but she felt the muscles in his tense, waiting for her next words. "My grandparents were dhampirs," she finally said. There. Now it was out there.

He was quiet, guiding her into an opulent dining room that was far too dark for so early in the day. A meal of cold roast beef and rolls was set out, along with a steaming teapot and matching cups.

He held out a chair for her, and she sank into it. He took a seat opposite her.

"Aren't you going to say anything?" she asked.

"I would, but I'm not sure what a dhampir is." He poured tea for each of them. His voice was still cautious. "Are you telling me that you're some sort of supernatural creature?"

Ada shook her head and helped herself to the food. "Descended from them," she said. "A dhampir is the offspring of a vampire and a human."

"Vampires can reproduce?" His hand hovered above the table, and a drop of tea splashed to the white damask cloth.

"Not very easily, and it's quite rare, but when the circumstances are right, newly turned male vampires can have children with human women." She looked at him across the table, and he set down his teacup, untouched. "Vampire and dhampir descendants can detect vampires. I get a headache when I'm near one, sharp pains right at my temples."

Weston entered the dining room before Max could reply. Ada tensed, unable to read Max's expression.

"Is the meal to your liking, Miss Burgess?" he asked.

She hadn't tasted the roast beef yet, but she was sure it would be delicious, better than anything she'd eaten in Europe so far. Anything that was home cooked was bound to be better than cheap vittles from crumbling food kiosks at airfields. "It's perfect, Weston, thank you."

"Weston, please sit down," Max ordered.

The butler did so, a curious look on his weathered face.

"You may think me mad, Weston, but I believe I know who may be responsible for Uncle James's murder," Max said. "But I would like to

61

hear your theories first. You must have read the papers."

Weston paled. "I identified his body myself, sir," He paused. "You may think me mad if I tell you what I think happened. I haven't mentioned it to the constables. They wouldn't believe me."

"Our theories may be similar. Weston, tell me."

"He was drained, sir." Weston's voice had dropped to a whisper.

Ada's suspicions were correct, and the broadsheet writers weren't that far off the mark with their theories.

"The papers my landlady saved for me mentioned that," Max said.

"There isn't any way anything natural could have done that. I didn't write the exact details in my letters to you because I didn't think you would believe me, either. I wouldn't have if I hadn't seen your poor uncle with my own eyes."

"Weston, would you believe me if I told you that I and Miss Burgess were attacked by vampires last night?"

Weston stilled, his gaze pinned on Max, who took a shaky sip of tea. He turned wide, terror-stricken eyes to Ada. "Sir, I would," he said, his voice a harsh gasp. "I wouldn't have six months ago, but now…"

"Do you think Uncle James was murdered by a vampire?" Max asked.

Weston nodded, his face still incredulous. "I do, sir."

"I'm a member of the American branch of the Searchers, out of the New York office," Ada said. "I'm descended from dhampirs, as I was explaining to Mr. Sterling just now. I'm human, but I can detect nearby vampires. I kill them for a living." Not a great one, but it kept a roof over her head, even if she had to share it. "I'm still waiting on word from the London office. There's a significant vampire infestation in London." She corrected herself. "There are infestations everywhere, actually, thanks to air travel. I met Mr. Sterling last night, as a vampire tried to eat him."

"Sir!" Weston looked at Max, horrified.

"She saved me," Max said. "I've never seen anything like it."

His voice thawed a few degrees, and Ada let herself relax slightly. Maybe he wouldn't be as disturbed about her ancestry as she thought.

Weston looked away. "It's a pity Miss Burgess couldn't have saved your uncle. Or if you were here, perhaps you could have persuaded him to give up his obsession with that *woman*." He nearly spat out the last word in his distaste.

Ada and Max stilled. "What woman?" Max said.

Weston looked distinctly uncomfortable. "Dr. Sterling's companion."

"Tell us about her," Max said urgently.

"I'd never seen anyone so besotted," Weston continued. "She seemed to adore Dr. Sterling. He was lonely, you know, since your aunt died. He kept mistresses occasionally, but…"

"I don't need those details, Weston."

The tiniest of sighs escaped Weston. "I suppose you don't. It may be easier for me to explain what I suspect led to your uncle's passing if I showed you his laboratory." Glancing at Ada, whose hand hovered over a roast beef sandwich, he added, "After Miss Burgess has finished her meal."

Well, if *that* didn't make her feel like even more of a gauche American… Max eyed her curiously across the table, but she didn't detect any fear or disgust from him, setting her a little more at ease. "I'll be quick," she said. "Why don't you tell us what you can? Believe me when I say that nothing you say will sound too insane."

"I imagine not, if you were attacked by vampires last night." Weston's expression grew more panicked, and his next words were rushed, as if he had been waiting for an eon to tell them and know they would be taken seriously. "Dr. Sterling was in love with a vampire himself."

CHAPTER
FIVE

M ax felt all the blood drain from his face at the butler's revelation. "Are you sure about that?"

But even before Weston nodded, Max knew the man was telling the truth. A vampire murdering his uncle made sense, and he already knew that the Scotland Yard would be of no help to him. What Max needed to find out was why.

His gaze turned to Ada, whose roast beef sandwich was still clutched in her hand. *A dhampir*, he thought. *She's descended from vampires*. For some reason, that bit of news didn't conjure up a wave of revulsion. Instead, it was actually a bit of a relief. She could sense monsters before they made themselves visible. Such a useful talent to have.

"I've never been more serious in my life, sir," Weston said. "I have your uncle's journal and research in his laboratory." The old man looked away from them, his throat frantically working. "I didn't show anything to the constables when they came round looking for clues. They would have thought Dr. Sterling mad and dismissed his journals, if not destroyed them. Or by some miracle, had they taken the vampire theory seriously, they might have gone off half-cocked into Wapping and burned everything down. Wapping is miserable enough as is without adding to it."

Something tugged at Max's memory. "Hold on," he said. "Ada, why didn't the London branch of your vampire hunting group investigate James's murder?"

"They may have," Ada said. "But all the branches have enough to investigate on their own without getting involved in other countries' problems. A single vampire attack in London wouldn't be worth sending a cable to New York. There were eight vampire infestations at home that I took care of last year. I doubt any London Searchers would know of them."

"Eight is a lot!"

"Actually, it's a lot less than usual," Ada said. "There was a huge blizzard in New York City last year, and no one left their homes if they couldn't help it. As a result, they had less chance of being sucked dry. The snow shut down the city for weeks. But like I said, eight deaths or even twenty vampire deaths isn't worth sending cables to other branches in a city that size. There's over a million people."

It sounded terribly inefficient to him, but he supposed there wasn't much in the way of improving communications between countries. Cables were the fastest way and their costs could add up quickly.

London's population was larger than New York's. How many people had died like Uncle James and their deaths gone unnoticed? James was a well-respected physician. His death certainly garnered far more attention than if he was one of the poor sods who haunted the East End.

Max stood up. "I'm going to James's laboratory. Weston, will it still be locked per usual?"

Weston shook his head. "I stopped locking it when I thought you were returning home."

Once again, guilt flared through Max for not responding to the butler's letters when he received them. "I apologize for not coming home when I was expected," he said quietly. "It was callous and selfish of me, and I will be forever grateful to your handling Uncle James's final affairs."

Weston rose as well. "Mr. Sterling, it was an honor to serve your uncle as long as I did. We were friends the last few years, or at least as close to friends as employer and employee can be. I miss him greatly."

Ada stood up to follow, although Max noticed she wrapped up the remains of her sandwich in a crisp white linen napkin and hid it in a pocket of her dress. She'd done the same with her scone that morning. He didn't say a word about it. She really did need a good meal or two, he decided. She was one of the most attractive women he ever met, but in the light of day he saw that she was a little too thin in the way that spoke of never having quite enough to eat.

James Sterling's laboratory was located in the attic, at the end of the corridor in the east wing and up two steep flights of stairs. The doors leading to it were now unlocked, something that never happened when James was still alive. Max had only been in there a handful of times since he was a boy, and his uncle was always careful to keep everything as tidy as he could in the unfinished room, his files locked away.

The laboratory this morning was organized as usual, save for a stack of journals and papers resting haphazardly in the center of the room's big wooden desk. Bookcases crammed with medical journals and loose papers lined the walls, and a large collection of scientific equipment that Max couldn't begin to name was clustered on top of a table in the corner. Despite the lab being located in the attic, the place was spotlessly clean, without a speck of dust to mar any surface. It was undoubtedly the result of Weston's fastidious care rather than the housekeeper.

"I took the liberty of reading some of his work," Weston confessed. Guilt traced his voice at the invasion of privacy.

"It's fine," Max said. "I mean that. I appreciate all that you've done for me. For James, as well," he added.

"Thank you, sir." Weston picked up a journal and held it out to Max. "Your uncle became infatuated with a young woman about six months ago," he said. "Cerys Hughes." The usually-dignified old man nearly spat out the name. "She was far too young for him, as I've said, but it wasn't just that. She was…" He searched for the right word. "Strange, sir. I noticed it straight away, although I couldn't put my finger on why I thought so."

"Vampire?" Ada immediately guessed. She sat down at James's desk and removed her pilfered sandwich from her skirt pocket.

"She was, yes." Despite his obvious grief and anger at his employer's murder, he still looked a little relieved to hear Ada say so. Max also noticed that he didn't so much as narrow his eyes at her eating in James's laboratory. "I cannot begin to tell you how it feels to know I'm not insane for thinking Dr. Sterling had fallen in love with a vampire."

"Tell me about her."

Ada's voice brooked no argument, and Max saw how she straightened in her chair, how her eyes took in the laboratory's details. She was looking for clues, he realized. She knew which questions to ask, where to look for answers. His respect for her ticked up another notch.

"At first, she only came around in the evenings," Weston said. "I didn't think anything unusual about that at first, because…" He hesitated.

"I'm from America, Mr. Weston. I also have two older brothers, one of whom chased anything in a skirt until he got married. You don't have to sugar coat what the men of the upper classes here get up to at night."

"It isn't unusual for the *demimonde* to travel in the evenings," Weston clarified. "But she started sleeping here during the daytime, and Dr. Sterling gave all of the staff strict orders to not so much as touch her bedchamber door, under threat of being sacked without a reference. Even me." He looked a little hurt.

"Did Dr. Sterling's health change at all? His personality?"

Weston nodded. "He looked much paler after Miss Hughes's first fortnight here. He was more irritable, snapped at all of us much more when before he didn't. Two of the maids quit after a month of Miss Hughes's stay, when Dr. Sterling began to change. She slept all day, every day, and only woke after sunset. He was short and rude with the staff, which he had never been before. Dr. Sterling started sleeping through the day, too, and eating liver in the evenings, before he woke up Miss Hughes, but his pallor and mood never improved.

69

He said his blood was sluggish, and liver would help revive it." His mouth puckered in distaste. "He drank cow's blood occasionally, as well, for the same reason."

"Liver's supposed to be good to eat after being bitten by a vampire," Ada said. "I'd rather just splash some holy water on the bite and be dizzy for the rest of the night. I hate liver. I don't care how good it's supposed to be for the constitution."

Weston leafed through one of the handwritten journals. "He was always interested in serology and hematology, you know, but his obsession increased after he met Cerys, to the neglect of all else. Shortly after she started spending her days here, Dr. Sterling stopped seeing patients. He bought that thing in the corner, the…" He thought for a few seconds, biting his lower lip. "Centrifuge." The machine in question was massive and looked heavy. Max didn't have a clue what it could do.

"He couldn't read enough about blood, he couldn't experiment on it often enough, and I don't mean with leeches. He took blood samples from all the household staff, his colleagues at the Royal Hospital, and I believe some of his patients." Weston opened a cabinet and pulled out a large wooden box and placed it on the desk. "These are all the samples he took. His microscope is over there." He nodded in the direction of the medical equipment.

Max lifted out a glass slide. Smeared on it were a few drops of blood, dried brown and starting to flake. He replaced it and picked up another to find the same thing. The slides were labelled with last names and dates.

"He said Miss Hughes was ill and he wanted to

find a cure for her," Weston said. "His methods are detailed in here." He tapped the journal.

"Did he tell you the nature of her disease?" Max asked.

"Only that she suffered from poor blood and fatal sensitivities to sunlight, silver, and garlic," Weston said. "After seeing what he looked like after he woke her up in the evenings, and his banishing garlic from the kitchen, I thought—well, I thought I was going mad when the idea that she was a vampire crossed my mind. Or he was, or possibly Miss Hughes was mad and he bought into her delusions."

"Did you ever find proof of her being a vampire?" Ada asked. She picked up one of the glass slides, examined the blood specks on it, and replaced it in its box.

"I never saw her feasting on Dr. Sterling, but he did have puncture marks on his neck occasionally."

"Younger vampires can't always seal wounds," Ada said. "It takes them time and practice to learn how to do it efficiently. Others don't do it just to be bastards."

Weston's face registered a trace of disgust. "I found her in the sitting room once, drinking a glass of something that looked like blood. Dr. Sterling said it was cow's blood, but I was not convinced it was." He looked at the stack of journals sadly. "I do not believe he ever came close to finding the cure for Miss Hughes's mysterious condition, but that didn't halt his obsession."

"Where's Miss Hughes now?" Ada asked.

"She passed away," Weston said.

Max was unsurprised at this bit of news, and Ada didn't seem rattled by it, either. "Do you know what happened?"

Weston nodded. "The details are in his journal. He was involved."

A ball of dread lodged itself in Max's stomach at this revelation. "Are you accusing my uncle of murder?"

"No!" Weston's protest was vehement. "Not at all. From what I read, they both knew there was a possibility that she would not survive his experiment. In fact, there's this." He opened the journal he held and removed a stiff sheet of paper, handing it to Max between two fingers, like he was afraid of the thing.

The writing was cramped, with many misspelled words and others crossed out, in an unfamiliar script.

To whoever it may concern,

I, Cerys Hughes, originally of Aberystwyth, and now of London, do solemnly swear that I understand what Dr. James Sterling is attempting to do to save my life. I do not wish to be a vampire, nor have I ever. I was transformed against my will by another vampire and came to Dr. Sterling when I discovered he researched diseases of the blood. I understand that the transfusion Dr. Sterling is attempting may kill me and do not hold him responsible. I love him with all my heart.

Cerys Hughes
8 December 1888.

He passed the note to Ada. "Cerys Hughes did not want to be a vampire," he said. "At least according to that letter. James was trying to help her. So he gave her a blood transfusion?"

"I'm not a doctor," Ada said, scanning the note, "But I can tell you right now that new blood won't cure vampirism. There isn't a way to reverse it."

"She was desperate," Max said. "I can read

that there. She was turned against her will." A flood of compassion for the deceased vampire flowed through him, surprising him. In the brief time he knew they existed, he had never considered that there could be vampires who didn't want to eat every human they came across.

"I didn't know what happened to her, exactly," Weston said. "But one night he brought her here to begin his experiment, and in the morning, he announced that she passed away."

"And there wouldn't be a body," Ada said. "Dead vampires crumble to ash when they die. Hell of a mess."

"But how would a blood transfusion kill a vampire?" Max asked.

Weston looked at the journal. "It's in here."

Max picked it up and leafed through it, finding the details of Cerys Hughes's final hours in one of the last journal entries. Nausea gripped him as he read the details. The transfusion started according to plan, then something happened.

Insanity overcame her as the final drops of blood were injected into her veins. She became a changed creature, the true monster she so feared becoming. I had to stake her to save my life. Now I wish I hadn't done it, that I let her turn me so we could have remained together.

He pushed the journal to Ada, tapping the passage with his finger.

Ada skimmed it, her eyes widening. "My God," she breathed. "He killed his lover."

Weston cringed.

"It was in self-defense," Max said. "Weston, I don't blame you for not turning over James's books and effects to the constables."

"There's nothing in here so far that tells us the name of the vampire who turned Cerys," Ada

73

said, flipping through the pages. "Mr. Weston, may I borrow this? I promise I'll return it."

"You may take whatever you need for your investigation," Weston said. "Please accept my gratitude for your help in this, Miss Burgess."

"Ada," she said automatically. She stood up and collected a few journals. Max did likewise. He noticed that she didn't seem interested in the rest of the laboratory or the equipment, but he could see why. Anything they could use to find out who murdered James would most likely be in his writings.

"I need to get in touch with the London branch as soon as possible. I'm expecting a cable soon," she said to Weston. "I contacted my employers in New York and asked them to deliver a reply here. Max said that would be all right."

"It is, and I shall deliver it to you as soon as it arrives. There is a telegraph office not two blocks from here if you need to send further correspondence. I can take care of anything you need."

"Thank you, Mr. Weston."

"Allow me to escort you to the study," he said. He helped himself to the books in her arms, which she gave up with a minimal amount of protest.

Max followed, closing the attic door behind them.

NOT FOR THE FIRST TIME, Ada wished she had some way of establishing immediate contact with the London office. *This is what I get for staking those vampires in Germany*, she thought. *All I wanted was to finally see Dresden, see where my grandparents came from.* So much for her attempt at a holiday. She should still be in Germany, or maybe taking a side trip to

Italy for the hell of it, not traipsing over half of Europe staking vampires. She couldn't just ignore them and go on her way when they crossed her path, though. Searchers had an obligation to seek out and destroy them, whenever they could.

She, like the rest of her family—all of the Searchers, in fact—would never be able to rest on their laurels when bloodsuckers were stomping around. She just wouldn't be so bitter about it had she had the opportunities to see a little more of the cities she found herself in, instead of constantly looking over her shoulder, far too short of money. It still rankled her that she had to sell the other two dresses she brought with her to buy a ticket to Bern.

At least her accommodations tonight were nice, she thought appreciatively as she took in her room again. She was still full from the sumptuous supper she and Max enjoyed in the dining room, insisting over Mr. Weston's apologies that the meal wasn't simple. It had four courses, she recalled. More meat and potatoes than she could remember in a long time. It had been spectacular.

She and Max had pored over Dr. Sterling's journals for the rest of the day after they investigated the laboratory, but there was little in there that could help them for the time being. There were pages and pages of notes and observations that detailed Cerys Hughes's condition while she slept, when she woke up hungry, what her disposition was like after eating. Pages written in a halting scrawl that matched Cerys's letter told the vampire's own sad story, of being attacked in her former employer's home and waking up three nights later after being pulled out of the Thames by a dockworker. She'd figured out what she was when her teeth elongated and she tried to eat the dockworker without thinking twice about it, but he'd pushed her away, screaming and bleeding.

Ada's heart broke for the poor woman. She hadn't asked for this; she was desperate when she came to Dr. Sterling, whose research in hematology and serology warranted a few inches of space in one of the London papers.

"I'm surprised she could read and write as well as she could," Max had remarked in the study that afternoon.

"You're surprised women can read?"

"This particular woman, yes. She was a housemaid."

Even though the comment wasn't directed at her, Ada still smarted at that. She came from a long line of working class folk, and everyone in her family was literate. "I can read and write," she said. Her spelling wasn't especially skilled, as the clerk in the telegraph office reminded her, but she'd never had a problem reading one of her beloved periodicals.

"I didn't insinuate you couldn't." Max didn't look up from the journal he was reading.

"Not all lower class women are completely illiterate," Ada said. "Maybe she learned in school, maybe her mother didn't want her opportunities to be limited."

Once again, she was reminded of their differences. Max would never understand the importance of opportunities, how devastating the lack of them could be. From her short time in Europe and Britain so far, she could tell plenty of other people didn't, either. She also knew the concept of improving one's station in life was decidedly American.

But Max, when he finally looked up at her, didn't have a trace of amusement or annoyance on his face. He looked almost—understanding? She hadn't expected that.

No, she had been expecting to tear his clothes off and have her way with him at the earliest opportunity before a vampire bite sidetracked them. Now, alone in her bedchamber, she wasn't sure that was going to happen. There was too much going on now for a sane person to think about *that*.

She gave a soft snort at that thought. Since when had she ever been a sane person? Sane people didn't cut short their holidays to stake things that went bump in the night. But tonight, she could finally get some rest.

The grandfather clock downstairs chimed ten times. Early for her; it was prime vampire hunting time, but she was tired from her lack of sleep the night before, and when she touched the spot on her neck where she was bitten, she still felt a twinge of pain. *Damn*, but that was a bad bite. She wanted to hunt tonight, but Max would probably want to go with her, and she couldn't have that. For now, it would be best to wait until she heard from the London branch and then stake vampires with one of their hunters.

Would Max still be awake? Ada toyed with the idea of knocking on his bedchamber door, see if he was amenable to… anything, really. She was surprised to find she really enjoyed his company and they hadn't even jumped into bed yet. That was unusual for her, and, she suspected, him too.

A soft knock at the door made a smile spread across her face. Maybe he was thinking along the same lines she was.

She opened it, unsurprised to see Max standing

in the corridor. His shirt collar was unbuttoned, his hair mussed like he'd run a hand through it. He looked disheveled and delicious, and she prayed he wasn't here just to talk about vampires.

His uncle was murdered, you twit. Of course he's thinking about vampires.

Well, that put a damper on her ardor.

"May I come in?" His voice held a hint of a promise, and Ada thought she might have been wrong about her initial impression.

"Please do."

He smiled at her formality, and held up a half-full bottle of port and a pair of glasses. "Nightcap?"

"I didn't know this was proper," Ada teased. "Are all Englishmen this welcoming to their lady houseguests?" She held the door open for him.

"No," he admitted, setting the bottle and glasses on a fussy little table. He poured an inch of port into each. "Just for you, Ada." He handed her one of the glasses and she clinked it against his in a silent toast.

For some reason, that made Ada feel a little giddy. He liked her, more than just as a possible lover, she hoped.

Why was she hoping for that? She'd never cared before. Why should she now?

"I hope I get a cable soon," she said, steering their conversation back to her thoughts. "I hate feeling so powerless, and not knowing where to go."

"You were all right staking vampires in Switzerland and France, though, were you not?" he asked. "From what you've told me, and what I saw at the Langham Hotel, you're capable of caring for yourself in strange places."

The compliment warmed her in a way the port didn't. "It's different when I'm not alone," she said.

"Am I a hindrance to you?" His eyes grew serious.

"No, more like a liability." She spoke without thinking, and saw hurt flash across his face. Damn! "That's not what I meant, Max. I mean that it's more dangerous hunting vampires when you're with someone inexperienced."

"I know what you meant." He looked down at his glass. "I understand the powerlessness, but more than that, I feel like an ass. I've been gallivanting around the world for years, ignoring the only living family I had, doing whatever I wanted, while Uncle James physicked the sick and you rid the world of monsters." His eyes, sad and defeated, met hers. "I've been thoughtless and selfish. I have to change that."

Ada shook her head. "You haven't. I know asses. I'm related to a few of them. Believe me, Max, you're not one of them."

Max sat down at the small table near the window, and Ada followed. "Tell me about your family," he said. "Why are you a vampire hunter, anyway?"

Ada exhaled noisily. "I didn't have much choice. Everyone in my family with the ability to sense vampires—which is all of us, so far—become Searchers."

"Searchers. That's an unusual name."

"It used to be *De Zoekers*. A secret society of vampire hunters from the Netherlands that began a couple hundred years ago. They followed vampires across the world to destroy them."

"And some your family was from the Netherlands?"

"No, they all came to America from Germany. That's why I was in Europe, actually. I was finally taking a trip to Dresden."

"Do you have family there?" he asked.

"None that I know of, but it's where my grandparents came from. The dhampir ones. I wanted to see where they started out. I'd been planning the trip for a couple of years." She sighed again. "I've hardly had a chance to actually travel. I didn't even make it to Dresden. I staked a pair of vampires when I landed in Berlin and I haven't stopped moving since."

"When this is over, I'll take you to Dresden."

Ada turned startled eyes to Max. "You can't be serious!"

"It's the least I could do," he said. "I owe you my life. You should be able to enjoy your holiday, without vampires imposing upon it. I know of a lovely hotel we could stay at while we're there."

He *was* serious, she realized. "I may take you up on that offer," she said carefully.

"Please do. I like Dresden. I think you'll like it, too." He swallowed the last of his port but didn't pour himself any more. "You haven't said yet why you became a Searcher."

"I did. I had to," she said again. "It's the moral thing to do when you have this ability."

"But if you didn't have to become one, what would you have done?"

Longing swept through Ada at the thought of her shelved dreams. Longing and regret. A bitter taste seeped into her mouth at the memories. "You'll laugh," she cautioned.

"I won't."

"I wanted to be a pilot. I started taking lessons when I was seventeen," she said. Her words were rushed; she wanted to get out the whole story before Max could find it amusing. "I'd been staking vampires for a couple years by then, and I was tired of it. I wanted something different. I'd always wanted to fly. I enrolled in courses at the New York Air Academy, but they're so expensive." And an unexpected nest of newly turned and very blood-lust-crazed vampires turned up in Chicago and required help from the New York branch. That mess had taken weeks to clean up, and a few vampires managed to escape for parts unknown anyway.

Max didn't laugh, though, just quietly regarded her through clear dark eyes.

"I wanted my own dirigible. I thought I could do both, use the dirigible business as a cover for hunting vampires. And see more of the world," she added wistfully. "I didn't have much of a choice when it came to joining the Searchers. When you're a Burgess and you have the sense, you join, no more questions."

"I would never laugh at you for that. It's an admirable dream, one that's still within your grasp."

She hadn't intended to tell Max all of that, and still felt embarrassment wash over her at her confession, even though his reply was encouraging. "Well, it's been eight years since my last lesson. What about you?" she asked, changing the subject. "Why don't you ever come back to England?"

"I've never liked staying in one place too long," he said. "I always wanted to travel and write, and I've done quite a lot of both. It's good that I did, because they were the only things I was ever proficient at. Uncle James pushed for me to follow him into medicine, but I lack both the inclination and the intelligence to do so."

"But you're so smart! You write so well!"

"A propensity for writing tall tales does not mean one is especially intelligent. I was an average student, at best. Certainly not someone who should be holding sharp knives over patients."

"What about your parents?" she asked.

"Passed on. My mother when I was born, my father in a submersible accident when I was a boy. I don't remember either of them."

He spoke of his parents' deaths matter-of-factly, as if they didn't bother him. Maybe they truly didn't, Ada thought. She missed her own parents fiercely, but she grew up with them. It had been ten years since her mother died of pneumonia, five since her father was hit by a carriage in Brooklyn. At least they hadn't died at the hands of vampires. Ada would always be grateful for that.

"No siblings?" she asked.

"None. It was just me and Uncle James, and we didn't always see eye-to-eye on a great deal of issues." He paused. "*Most* issues, actually. He thought I was wasting my potential, as he called it. When he wasn't busy in his laboratory or the hospital, of course. I left England as soon as I reached my majority and rarely returned. I last saw him four years ago." He turned sad eyes to Ada. "I'm unsure if I regret his passing so much as regretting that we could never seem to have a relationship. I'm mourning what could have been, not the man himself. Does this make me a terrible person?"

"Of course it doesn't. You can't help how you feel, just how you act on your feelings."

"The least I can do is find out why he died." His gaze turned flinty, determined.

"I'm happy to help you with that. Staking vampires is what I do best. Well, *one* of the things I do best."

Damn! She hadn't meant to let that innuendo slip out. The man was pouring his heart out to her, and now he was going to think that all she wanted was something carnal from him.

She did, but so far, she just liked him. She cared about his opinions and feelings, which wasn't something she usually expected to do with her lovers, nor did she expect it in return.

Max's eyes darkened at her words, and she thought she might not have misstepped, after all. "What else do you do best?" he asked. An undercurrent, thick and darkly exciting, laced his voice.

Awareness rippled through Ada, and all thoughts of her aborted trip to Dresden and vampires flew from her mind. She was remembering the Max who had kissed her so thoroughly outside the Langham Hotel last night—was it only last night?—and she uttered a quick, silent prayer that his mind might be on the same page as hers right now.

"That information is need-to-know," she said, her voice light.

"What if I told you I needed to know?" His mouth hovered inches from her ear, breath tickling her skin, and a shudder wracked through her at the teasing sensation.

Rational thought fled her mind. "I'd probably —oh, God!—agree." His tongue had found the sensitive spot just under her ear, where her pulse beat in an increasing tattoo. She turned her head, her lips finding his, and let him pick her up and carry her back to the bed dominating the room. He kneeled over her, leaving a trail of kisses over her neck where her stupid high-necked dress didn't cover her skin.

He had flicked open her dress's buttons and

peeled it away from her body before a sobering thought derailed her ardor. "Max, stop."

Immediately his fingers stilled, and he sat up, balanced on his knees on either side of her. "Are you all right?" he asked, alarm lacing his words.

"I am," she said. "It's *you* I'm worried about."

What was it about this man that made her care about him? She'd rescued other men from vampires before and sent them back to their lives without another thought about them. She'd done the same with other lovers, as well.

Ada didn't like caring about other people. It made things so much more complicated.

Still, she forced herself to explain. "I just—I want you to want this," she said softly. She swallowed, trying to dislodge the lump in her throat and failing. "You're grieving, and I don't want you to do something you might regret later on."

He touched his thumb to her lips. "I don't think that will happen, Ada."

"I don't want to be a distraction, Max," she said.

He shook his head. "You aren't. Ada, I don't know what it is, except that it's not all because you saved me last night, but I think the world of you. I want you no matter the circumstances."

The words warmed her, not just in body but in soul. It wasn't a feeling she was accustomed to, but she liked it. "All right," she said.

"All right, I can stay the night with you?"

Anticipation sent tingles down her spine that radiated through her body. Somehow, she had the notion that spending one night together might not be enough. "Yes," she said, not bothering to try to hide the breathiness of her reply.

His eyes sparkled, and a small smile quirked the

corner of his mouth. His nimble fingers resumed unbuttoning her dress, revealing the corset she'd been damning since arriving in Europe. He pushed her dress down her body and tossed it over the side of the bed, and she didn't look to see where it landed.

Max unhooked her corset, pulling the sides apart. Ada involuntarily rolled her shoulders, releasing some of the stiffness in her back it caused. She drew in a deep breath for the first time in hours. "Thank you," she said.

His lips hovered an inch above hers. "What for?"

"Taking off that damn thing. I hate it."

"You don't wear one in New York?" He actually looked a little intrigued at the idea.

"When I do, it isn't as restrictive as this," she said. "It isn't nearly as uncomfortable."

He trailed a line of kisses down her throat to her collarbone, and any remaining thought about her corset fled her mind. He pushed her well-worn shift up her body, pulling it over her head and throwing it somewhere in the vicinity of her corset. His hands skimmed over the pale flesh of her belly next, until they landed at the tops of her thighs, where her stockings were tied with mismatched ribbons.

"Wait," she said.

He paused, fingers poised over one stocking. "Ada?"

She sat up and reached for his shirt, grabbing a fistful of cloth. "Why am I the only one getting naked?" she asked.

"Because you look much better undressed than I do."

She giggled at that, because she knew it wasn't

true. She'd lost weight since starting her journey through Europe, and besides that, she had scars. Scars from fighting with vampires, old marks from childhood scrapes. But as she unbuttoned Max's shirt and his eyes never left her face, she could tell he wasn't seeing her imperfections, and that warmed her in a way she hadn't experienced before.

He really did care about her. She believed that now.

His shirt unbuttoned, she pushed it off his shoulders. He stripped off his undershirt before she could, and she was finally able to feast her eyes on his bare skin. He was, as she suspected the first time she saw him accompanying Lisette Babineau, just as firm as he looked.

A puckered, circular scar marred one shoulder, small and dark. "What's that?" she asked, running her fingers over it.

"I had a fencing accident when I was in university," he said. "It turns out I'm terrible at defending myself and holding a foil at the same time."

"How badly did it hurt?"

"Not as much as vampire fangs, but it was certainly more than a pinch."

Ada ran her tongue over the spot, savoring Max's sharp intake of breath at the sensation. Her hands slid down his chest to his trousers and deftly unhooked the buttons there. Her hand brushed over the hard bulge of his erection, and she slipped her hand inside his loosened trousers to stroke his cock.

He groaned in response, pushing up to meet her hand. His mouth crashed down on hers, tongue sweeping into her mouth. The sensation sent waves of heat wracking through her body, starting at her dampening sex and fanning out.

She broke away from him long enough to whisper, "We need to take these off." She pushed at the fabric of his trousers, but he was faster. He slid them down his hips and kicked them away, along with his drawers.

He leaned over her, mouth inches from a nipple stiffening in the cool air, but she halted him, her hands on his shoulders. "Wait," she said.

Max paused, a quizzical look on his face.

Ada sat up, and he did likewise, resting on his knees. Her gaze roved over him. "I just wanted to take a look first."

He grinned, without a trace of self-consciousness. "What do you think?"

Ada ran her finger over the center of his chest, along the light dusting of hair that arrowed down his body, brushing over his cock with a teasing, feather-light touch.

He closed his eyes for a second, fighting for control.

She wrapped her hand around him, feeling desire pulse through the delicate skin. She leaned down, licking the head. His hands fisted in her hair.

She took him in her mouth, her tongue sliding over him.

He thrust into her, a moan escaping his throat. "Mother of God," he said, the words sounding pained. But he urged her on, guiding her as she sucked him.

"Damn." He pulled away, and she looked up. Desire still smoldered in his eyes, and he pushed her back against the pillows, moving her still-stockinged legs apart. He settled between them, his lips finding her neck. "Ada, can I try something with you?" His breath tickled her ear.

"Yes." Her voice was breathless and her heart pounded so hard she thought he must have noticed. His erection bobbed against her hip and she strained upward, wanting it inside her.

"Tell me if you want me to stop."

"I don't think that's going to happen, but all right," she said.

"Raise your arms."

The command in his voice sent a shiver of anticipation down Ada's spine, and she obeyed. He guided her hands to the posts on either side of her head.

"Keep them there," he said.

He rolled one stocking down her leg, then the other, and Ada immediately knew what he planned. Excitement coiled in her belly and she kept her hands at the headboard.

He loosely tied one wrist to one of the headboard's wooden posts with a stocking. He hesitated with the second, a question in his eyes.

"Do it," she said.

Max tied her other wrist to the headboard. She flexed her hands; they were loose enough for her to slip out of without help if she wanted to.

Not that she did.

She strained upward, her lips crashing into his. He settled between her legs, one hand gently stroking her wet sex. He slipped a finger inside her. She moaned, desperate for more. "Max, *please*," she whimpered.

"Please, what?" he asked. He added another finger, sliding back and forth inside her in a maddening rhythm that did nothing but make her burn hotter.

"Max, I want you. I need more than this."

He withdrew his hand and kissed her, teasing her lips apart. She felt his cock nudge against her, and she wrapped her legs around his waist, urging him on.

Finally, he slid into her with an agonizing slowness, drawing a sigh of relief from her lungs.

She shifted, adjusting to the heavy feel of him inside her.

"Better?" he asked. He stroked her arm with a fingertip, but otherwise kept himself perfectly still.

Ada moved her hips, trying to encourage him. "Max, I need more," she said.

"What do you say?"

Her voice was pleading, desperate. "Please."

Without another word, he began to move, filling her and withdrawing in a tempo that sent pleasure radiating from her core. The rest of the world blotted out; all she could focus on was the incredible sensation of Max fucking her and the sight of him over her, the intensity written across his face. Her stockings rubbed against her wrists, not an unpleasant feeling, and she gripped the bedposts they were tied to.

Her hips jerked involuntarily against him as she ached for a release. Max's hand moved between their bodies, finding that aching spot and flicking it with his fingers. "Do that again," Ada said.

He did, and seconds later she came apart, the orgasm tearing a cry from her throat. Max didn't stop, but sped up, and she saw he was close as well. His mouth covered hers, and with a muffled cry he pulled out of her, spilling on the blanket.

He sagged against her, face buried in her neck. His breath came fast and harsh against her skin, his heartbeat moving in time with hers. He reached up and untied her wrists, massaging her skin.

"Max," she whispered.

"Mmm?" He rolled over to his side, taking her with him. His eyes met hers, and he brushed a curl out of her face.

"I don't know what that was, but…" She gave a shaky laugh. "Wow."

"That was the best I've ever had," he said bluntly.

There really wasn't any other way to describe what just happened except that. "For me, too." She snuggled into his chest. "Stay the night with me?"

He dropped a kiss to her lips. "Whatever you want."

CHAPTER
SIX

A thin stream of sunlight broke through a gap in the drapes, and Max was glad to see it. He turned over on his side to the woman sleeping beside him, russet hair in disarray over her pillow. She managed to snag most of the bedclothes in her sleep, but he didn't mind.

Hopefully Ada would receive a response to her cable from the day before. With a sinking feeling, he realized such a message might mean she would leave him while she went off with real vampire hunters to investigate Uncle James's murder, and he wasn't ready to let her go just yet. Perhaps she would let him go with her.

He meant what he said the night before. He would take her to Dresden, show her the city, and help her learn more about her ancestry there.

Max let his imagination roam in a way he rarely did outside of his writing. He'd never been to America. It was high time he remedied. He could rent a dirigible and hire a pilot and they could travel together. She could finally receive her flying license and sail the skies the way she always wanted to, traveling and ridding the world of monsters.

He wanted to do that with her. The idea scared him a little, but so had traveling the first time he boarded a dirigible for the Continent. He liked doing things that scared him.

She shifted in bed, and her dark eyes opened, blearily taking him in in undressed glory. "Good morning." She yawned. Her eyes widened, and she was suddenly awake. "I've stolen the covers, haven't I?"

"I don't think you intended to do it, but I'm warm enough."

She unwrapped herself from the cocoon of blankets and pushed some over to him. "I'm sorry," she said.

He shoved the blankets away and reached for her instead. "No apologies necessary."

She responded eagerly when he kissed her, all thought of cables and vampires again evaporating from his mind.

It was past ten when they finally made their way to the dining room for breakfast. Max noted Ada's nose gave a barely perceptible wrinkle of distaste at the sight of the teapot. "I regret that I do not have any coffee on hand," he said apologetically.

"Tea is fine. But please pass the sugar."

He did so, and tried to suppress his own shudder of revulsion as she dropped three spoonfuls in her tea. He really should get her some coffee, if only so he didn't have to see a perfectly good cup of tea maligned in such a way.

Weston strode into the dining room. "Sir, Miss

Burgess, a messenger has arrived with a telegram." He held out an envelope addressed to Ada.

She stood up so quickly her hip hit the edge of the table. "Damn," she muttered. She accepted the envelope. "Thank you, Mr. Weston." She tore it open.

"What does it say?" Max asked.

"It's instructions to meet one of the London Searchers," she said, laying the cable on the table. Weston and Max leaned over, reading it. "No address for the headquarters yet, but that's what I expected." It was too dangerous to send the exact address.

Meet Seecombe stop 7 Sisters 3 pm today stop

"What's the Seven Sisters?" Ada asked.

"It's a railway station," Max said. "We can take a steam cab there to meet this Seecombe for three o'clock. Do you think we should look for Cerys Hughes's former employer first, though?"

Ada thought for a few seconds. If she was alone, she would look for the vampire's employer, but Max was something of a liability at the moment. She had no doubt that with some training and experience, he could probably be a good Searcher. Regular people without the sense were very much part of the organization and deeply valued. But he didn't have either of those, and she was reluctant to put him in a situation he wasn't qualified to handle. She was unsure how to navigate London most efficiently. She was also tired of doing all of this alone. It was nice to have a companion for once. It was abysmally selfish of her, but his company, in and out of bed, was addictive.

She realized Max was still waiting for an answer. "I think we should meet Seecombe first," she said, noting that he brightened when she said *we*.

"He'll know London, and you have the manners and polish to maybe get us a meeting with Cerys's old employer."

"I'll have you know that my table manners were a never-ending source of embarrassment for my uncle and Weston until I was an adult."

Ada chanced a glance at Weston, who offered only the barest of nods.

"Well, I'm an ignorant American. In my family, if you don't pick your teeth at the table, you're high class." She shot a grin his way, but he didn't return it.

"Ada," he said quietly. He touched her mouth with his thumb, and she nearly melted into his hand. "I don't ever want you to think I look down on you, or anyone, because of circumstances beyond their control. I don't care about class. I just like *you*."

Her breath caught, and she felt tears unexpectedly well up in her eyes. She blinked, willing them away and hoping Max hadn't noticed. She hadn't known she needed to hear those words until now. They made her feel a little less out of her element. She swallowed the lump in her throat, and when she spoke, her voice was steady. "Thank you."

"I meant what I said about Dresden, too."

She nodded. "I'd love to go to Dresden with you."

"And I want to help you in any way I can with the vampires," he said. "Teach me whatever you think I should know."

She laughed. "Holy water, wooden stakes, crucifixes, garlic. All those old legends have some truth to them. Although the garlic isn't always as helpful as they say, because it's really only effective against younger vampires. It still doesn't hurt to keep a few cloves in your pockets, though. Or even eat it if you can." She paused. "I don't mind the smell that comes off after you eat it, but I've also been surrounded by vampire hunters all my life."

"I shall obtain some garlic, then. And I believe my mother had at least one or two crosses in her jewelry collection."

Ada nodded again. "It's a good idea to keep one on you. But you have to remember that what makes them effective against vampires is the faith behind them, rather than the cross itself. You have to believe in their power."

"I'm not terribly religious," he admitted. "I was baptized, but…"

"It still works," she said. "Of course, someone who has faith in the religion behind sacred objects will have better luck warding themselves against vampires, but knowing and having faith in a cross's power itself is still effective."

"I'll look for those crosses now. I assume you have one?"

"A couple." She removed a small copper cross from her pocket, one that had belonged to her mother. It was tarnished and bore a few nicks and scratches, the result of being passed down through the generations. "I have another silver one in my bag that I usually wear around my neck."

He held out his arm. It was a gesture she didn't think she would ever stop finding sweet. "Come with me, and we'll find those crosses."

THE AIR in the train station tasted a little dirty, and the day was uncharacteristically humid for April in England. Beads of sweat popped out of Max's forehead, and Ada looked a little flushed, as well. They waited on the train platform, scanning the crowd. There had been no other contact from the London Searchers, so they had no idea what Seecombe looked like, or where exactly where they would be met. So they waited on the northwest platform, hoping he or she might pick them out.

At ten minutes past three, a tall young man, perhaps a year or two older than Max's thirty, stopped by them. Impeccably dressed in a dark gray suit and matching hat, he tilted his head in greeting at Ada, ignoring Max. "Miss Burgess?"

"Yes?" She replied expectantly.

"Samuel Seecombe, from the London head-quarters."

"Adaline Burgess, from the New York branch, but I guess you already know that. This is my friend, Maximilian Sterling. We've been working together for the last few days."

Seecombe turned to Max, the tiniest twitch of his lips the only sign of the other man's distaste. "Are you a Searcher, Mr. Sterling?" He already knew Max wasn't a Searcher. His expression said as much.

"No," Max said. "I only recently met Miss Burgess after she saved my life from a vampire."

"It was mutual," Ada said. "I was bitten by a different vampire the same night, and he ran out to a church to get some holy water. He's the reason I'm not disfigured or dead right now."

"My understanding is that the American Searchers hold secrecy just as highly as your British counterparts."

"We do," Ada said. "But the circumstances that Max and I met under were, um…" She was clearly rattled by Seecombe's irritation at Max's presence.

"Extenuating," Max said.

"Yes, that." She shot him a grateful look.

Max tried to reassure Seecombe. "You don't have any reason to worry that I'll be telling vampire stories to everyone I meet. Ada asked me to accompany her to the house of a newly turned vampire my late uncle was trying to help, and of course we want your assistance."

Seecombe nodded, but still narrowed his eyes at Max. "We'll go to headquarters first," he said. "We will have to sit down in a more secure area and compare notes. There has been an increase in vampire activity in London recently. In particular more new vampires are turning up." He offered his arm to Ada. "It's a short train ride away, if you'll come with me."

Ada's dark eyes flitted back and forth between Seecombe and Max. Max exhaled a small sigh of relief when she placed her hand on his arm. "Of course," she said smoothly. "Lead on, Mr. Seecombe."

The other man didn't miss the slight and lowered his arm. "Follow me."

Once onboard the train, Max ignored Seecombe's glower and enjoyed Ada's reaction to sights outside. It was the first time he saw her enjoy herself in London outside of the bedroom. "My brothers would love this," she said. "I wish I could take a photograph or something to remember it."

"I can arrange for that," Seecombe offered. "I can take you to buy postcards to send home, if you like. How long do you plan to stay in London, Miss Burgess?"

"I'll be helping out with your vampire infestation and then making my way back to Germany." Max noted that she didn't ask Seecombe to call her

Ada, and he couldn't suppress a tiny, obnoxious sense of satisfaction at that. Which shouldn't be necessary, he told himself. She had chosen to spend the night with him and made it clear to Seecombe that she was returning to Germany, a trip Max would bankroll.

Judging from the narrowing of Seecombe's eyes, Max could tell the other man already disliked him. But he would *not* get sucked into a pissing match with Samuel Seecombe.

The train ride to Palace Gates station was quiet, although he could tell Ada picked up the tension between him and Seecombe and was dying to comment on it. She remained quiet though, until Seecombe hailed a steam cab outside the train station and all of them climbed in. The driver barely acknowledged their presence and, as soon as Seecombe gave him the destination, flipped up the rusted metal grate behind his seat, separating the driver's cab from the seats in back.

"I've never worked with a foreign branch," Ada said. "It didn't really occur to me how secretive the Searchers are until I arrived in Europe. Everyone I know back home is involved with the group in some way. I've been working on my own since I arrived until now."

"Mr. Sterling, are you interested in becoming a Searcher?" Seecombe's voice was exceedingly polite, but Max could still detect the condescension dripping from it.

"I lack the sensory ability of Searchers to be of much use." Max hated to admit that, but it was pointless to lie. He couldn't be a very effective Searcher.

"Regular people are still helpful to the organization," Seecombe said. "Searchers with the sense are far fewer in number, and we're shrinking still. The London branch is working on methods to ferret out vampires without the use of sensory abilities. Miss Burgess, I assume you have the ability?"

Ada nodded. "Descended from German dhampirs."

"My family is officially German as well, but there is quite a bit of Balkan ancestry that we don't discuss." Seecombe shot a quick grin Ada's way.

Ada offered a weak smile in return.

An uncomfortable silence settled over the cab. Their driver, either oblivious to their discussion or simply uncaring of it, swore at something in the road and lit his pipe with one hand. Smoke drifted into the back of the cab.

Ada coughed slightly.

Seecombe looked out the window. "We're almost there. Miss Burgess, are the rest of your family Searchers?"

Ada nodded. "My brothers are, and the one who managed to convince someone to marry him is, as well. Edgar and Francis are rough sorts, but I guess all of us are."

"There aren't so many female Searchers in England," Seecombe said. "It's unusual."

So *that's* what this was about, Max realized. Seecombe didn't know any women in their organization. Ada was a novelty to him. He relaxed a little.

The cab left them at an unfamiliar intersection, and from there Seecombe led them to a small, nondescript brick house on an ordinary street. A cross was nailed to the front door, which was festooned with four locks of differing metals and sizes. Max also noticed tarnished silver strips lining the doorjamb and threshold, but other than those features, it looked like any other house in a working class neighborhood.

Seecombe unlocked the door and opened it. It was dark inside, the drapes pulled closed. They walked past gas-powered sconces lining the walls until they reached a study. They passed by a couple of other men on the way, as well-dressed as Seecombe, but the other man didn't introduce them. They looked at Ada and Max with a little curiosity, but turned back to their newspapers and books. It must be a quiet day for the London Searchers.

Seecombe sat down behind the desk dominating the study, gesturing for Ada and Max to take seats in front of it. Max noted that a head of garlic was strung up in front of the covered window. Seecombe saw him staring at it.

"We keep the windows covered in the event a vampire looks through them and tries to enthrall a Searcher through the glass," he said by way of explanation. "Searchers are usually less susceptible to being enthralled, but of course we're not totally immune." He opened a desk drawer and removed some foolscap and a pencil, then looked at them expectantly. "Now, tell me everything you know."

～

"I HATE THEM."

It was nearing dusk, and Ada and Max were finally able to leave the Searcher headquarters. Ada gripped her satchel more closely as she and Max walked away from the brick house, even though there was little danger of vampires this early in the evening.

"I felt the same," Max said. "I assume the New York branch is structured differently?"

"Of course! There are over fifty in New York, and that still isn't enough! There are so few of them here! There are ten Searchers in London. *Ten*! No wonder there's an infestation here, Max. Everyone's so snobby about letting in and training other people without the sense or, God forbid, allow *women* who have it into their little club." She looked at the street before them without really seeing anything. "They can research steam-powered and electric methods all they want to track down vampires, it still isn't the same as having people go out there and looking for them. They're doing everything they can to keep their hands from getting dirty. *Bastards*." She nearly spat out the last word. "What a waste of time. Max, I'm sorry for dragging you out here." She sighed in frustration.

She knew the reason Seecombe was so fascinated with her was due to her being a woman with the vampire sensory ability. Even though Max wasn't a jackass obsessed with class didn't mean others from his station weren't. Ada was unmarried and could sense vampires in a city where people with that ability were dying out. Men like Samuel Seecombe viewed women like her as broodmares.

All Samuel Seecombe had done was write down everything they had seen so far in Paris and London. Ada told him about tracking down vampires through Germany, Switzerland, and France, about following Lisette Babineau and Max, about slaying that particular vampire and Max taking her in. She left out their bedroom activities, but she didn't think Seecombe didn't at least suspect something might be going on between them. It wasn't his concern, anyway. Ada never apologized for her personal affairs, and she wasn't going to start now.

"There's no need to apologize." Max's voice was calm, reassuring. "Ada, what I've seen of you so far—you know what you're doing. You can sort this out and I'll help you any way I can. You have my word."

"Thank you." Ada sighed, appreciating his help but unable to smother her irritation at the rest of the situation. "Let's go track down Cerys Hughes's last known employer."

ACCORDING to James Sterling's notes, Cerys Hughes worked for the Halsall family, who, it turned out, owned Great Britain's largest manufacturer of dirigible engines. The Halsalls' home was a new, massive, sprawling affair in Knightsbridge, a modern monstrosity that looked garish and tastelessly overdone compared to its dignified, stately neighbors.

They had already decided that there wasn't much need for a cover story. Max would tell Mr. Halsall that his former employee was a friend of his late uncle and he was searching for more information about her. There had been no mention of Cerys Hughes's death in any of the broadsheets, let alone the canal worker she tried to eat after turning, but that didn't mean the Halsalls or their staff didn't know what she was. It was important to proceed with caution.

A dour-faced woman of indeterminate age answered the door. "Good afternoon," she said stiffly. "What can I help you with?"

"We wish to speak with Mr. or Mrs. Halsall,"

Max said. He smiled at her in a way that usually had a positive effect on women, but didn't appear to have an effect on her.

"No solicitors," she said. She motioned to close the door, but Max held it open. She turned an appalled gaze to him. "What is the meaning of this?"

"It's of utmost importance that I speak to Mr. or Mrs. Halsall," he said. "It's concerning one of their former employees."

"If it's about a former employee you can speak to me," the woman said. "I'm the housekeeper and hire them all."

"We're looking for information about Cerys Hughes in particular."

Her eyebrows arched in surprise. "I see."

"You know her, then?" Ada said.

"We weren't friends, but of course we were acquainted, working here together. She ran off in the middle of the night, didn't even have the decency to stick around and let me sack her properly."

"What for?" Ada asked.

The woman paused and looked out at the street, as if afraid they were being watched. "Step into the foyer," she said. "There's no use carrying on here where the neighbors can see us and judge the Halsalls common more than they already do. You'll get five minutes out of me," she warned them, "and only in the foyer, on the rug. I've just cleaned the floor."

Such a pleasant woman. They stepped inside, and the housekeeper closed the door behind them. "I'm Maximilian Sterling, and this is my companion, Adaline Burgess."

"Pleased to meet you," Ada said, although she sounded anything but.

"Canadian?" the housekeeper asked.

"No, ma'am, American."

"My son ran off to Montreal last year and I haven't heard from him since. Are *you* familiar with Montreal?"

"I can't say I am."

"I suppose it's too far away. I'm Mrs. Poole." She offered Max a brittle smile, and he suspected the action didn't come to her easily. "I made the mistake of hiring Cerys Hughes last year. She started off all right, but a few months ago she started behaving in a way unfit for the Halsall home."

"How so?" Max pressed.

"Why do you care?" Mrs. Poole asked, an edge to her voice.

Max sighed. He removed ten shillings from his coat pocket and slipped it into the housekeeper's hand.

The coins disappeared into a pocket of her starched apron. "You're not with the constables, are you?"

"No," said Ada, her accent highlighting that fact.

"Cerys took up with that ne'er-do-well duke's nephew, whatever his name is. Quinn, that's it. Edward Quinn." Mrs. Poole's lips tightened as she recalled the details. "There was always something wrong with that boy, but now he's just… strange, I suppose. More than that." For the first time, the housekeeper finally showed signs of something other than anger or irritation. Her next words were spoken with a waver in her voice. "I'd swear that boy turned evil, if I didn't know any better."

Mrs. Poole was afraid of Edward Quinn.

"Cerys lived here, of course. She shared a room with one of the maids who I had to sack later on for something else. Edward Quinn started coming round, late at night, and Cerys let him on one evening. I found them…" She looked pained, and embarrassment flitted across her weathered face. "Well, we all know what kind of relations occur between men and women. They were still mostly dressed, but he was biting her neck."

She looked mortified, and beneath that, afraid.

She didn't want to believe what she really saw that night.

"That must have been awkward." Ada's voice uncharacteristically lacked a teasing note to the words.

"I told her to leave immediately," Mrs. Poole said. "What choice did I have? She cried. They all do. Just took off in the night, and I never saw her again. She left all her belongings behind, too. Couldn't even let me sack her properly."

It was chilling to think about what really happened that night, but Max knew that Mrs. Poole wouldn't believe any stories he told her about vampires or their thralls. "Do you know more about this Edward Quinn?" Max asked.

She waved a thin hand. "His uncle is the duke of something or other and rarely here. Greenwood, perhaps. Spends his time in the country, I believe. I don't know exactly, I'm unfamiliar with *Debrett's*. The nephew lives near here, in the duke's home. Only comes out at night." With those words, Mrs. Poole actually shuddered.

"Thank you," Max said. "You've been very helpful and we apologize for bothering you." He reached for the doorknob.

"You haven't told me why you're looking for Cerys," Mrs. Poole said.

Max paused, exchanging a glance with Ada.

"She was a dear friend of my uncle's," he finally said. "They both passed away recently."

"You're telling me Cerys is dead?"

"I am."

Her lips pursed in distaste. "Good riddance to bad rubbish."

Good Lord!

Ada merely gawked at her, speechless.

He and Ada left the house without another word to the housekeeper. "What the hell is wrong with your country?" Ada demanded.

"Where shall I start?"

"With the housekeepers. Between Mrs. Poole and the bitch who owns your flat, they're real pieces of work."

"That's the nicest thing you've ever said about Mrs. Boggs. Although I should remind you that she's actually my landlady."

"I can be nice when the need arises. Max, let's find this duke's nephew and see why he's changing maids into vampires."

CHAPTER
SEVEN

It was necessary to take a steam cab back to Max's house in Mayfair, and consult with his uncle's tattered copy of *Debrett's Peerage* to gain an idea of who the vampire might be. Ada hadn't heard of the book until that day.

"Are you listed in it?" she asked Max. They were in his uncle's study, surrounded by shelves and shelves of books.

He shook his head. "My father and James were cousins of an earl whom I've never met. I'm so far down the line of succession that I wouldn't be listed. Besides, this copy is at least twenty years old."

"Hopefully there'll still be something to tell us who Lord Greenwood's nephew is." Ada leafed through the pages, fascinated at the sheer number of names, the people who were important enough to be listed in such a book by the sheer dumb luck of the circumstances of their births. People who hadn't done anything to deserve such privilege.

She handed it to Max, who flipped through the pages. "There isn't a Greenwood who would fit the criteria," he said. "There's a Lord Greenstone. The current title belongs to Oliver Quinn, or it did at the time this was printed."

"Edward Quinn's uncle," Ada said automatically.

"It's probable." Max set the book aside. "Ada, what do we do now?"

"I send a cable to New York telling them the London branch is utterly worthless and I'll have to stake the bastard myself." She sighed, knowing the panic and outrage such a cable would provoke. "I may have to ask for Samuel Seecombe's help, even though I don't want to."

"I'll help any way I can." Max's voice was serious.

"I know you will, and I know you understand how dangerous this is." Ada had been thinking about how she was going to handle this situation since they left the London headquarters. As inefficient as they appeared to be, they were aware of the growing vampire population in the city and were taking steps to eradicate the problem. Now that she knew who the likeliest culprit behind the recent turnings was, she could handle the execution. Ideally, she would be doing it alone, but she knew Max would never tolerate that.

She had a feeling he would be sticking around her even after she left London. After his promised trip to Dresden, even. She didn't know exactly how to quantify her growing feelings for him, only that she wanted to keep him in her life as long as she could. Ada had long preferred to keep her relationships with men uncomplicated. In the space of a few days Maximilian Sterling had her reconsidering that notion.

"We'll need more stakes," she said. "I have mine, but you'll need to defend yourself, too."

"Will ordinary wood do, or does it need to be blessed?" Max was probably thinking of how crucifixes were most effective.

"Ordinary wood is fine, as long as it's sturdy. I think my stakes were originally made from table legs, but they've been in the family so long I'm not very certain."

"I have furniture that will suffice. It's ugly anyway."

"It also wouldn't hurt to eat some garlic before we go out. I think we still have enough holy water. Damn it!" she said harshly.

"Are we missing something?"

"No." She rubbed her temples, feeling an ache there that had nothing to do with vampires nearby. "I really hate putting you in this position, Max. Even if we only run across Edward Quinn and he's a newly turned vampire as I suspect, this is still dangerous. I wish we could go during the day to his hiding place and stake him in his sleep." That would be ideal for all vampire executions, except the bastards were incredibly clever at concealing their daytime sleeping spots. They wouldn't live for centuries without doing so. So Ada and the rest of the Searchers were forced to work at night.

As if he could read her mind, Max asked, "How often do you find them during the day?"

She shrugged. "Not often. Cemetery crypts are popular places for them to sleep, but we can't very well barge into them with stakes and terrify innocent people who are just trying to bury their grandmothers in peace. Sometimes they take up in a private home or shop cellar or attic, and we can't always break in there, either. You've also seen the mess a dead vampire can make." She remembered the messes left in the Langham Hotel. As far as she and Max knew there hadn't been a public outcry over the oily remains of Madame Babineau, and if the incident *had* made the papers, Seecombe certainly would have informed her, if Silas Weston hadn't first. She was lucky that night, in more ways than one.

"This is what we're going to do," she said. "We'll have to tell the London branch what we're doing, because it's the polite thing to do."

"Did you tell the local branches when you were staking vampires in Germany and Switzerland?"

"There wasn't enough time. I sent cables back to New York so they could get in touch with those offices, but I didn't deal with anyone else. This is different," she said. "I'm not passing by an alley at night, sensing a vampire, and doing the right thing. I'm making a plan to execute a vampire, maybe someone who comes from a well-known family, in another branch's territory. A branch that knows I'm here. We find Edward Quinn, stake him, get justice for your uncle and Cerys Hughes, then I can finally take that trip to Dresden."

"*We* take that trip to Dresden," Max said.

She smiled, delighted that he intended to keep his promise. "*We* go."

Max paused, at an uncharacteristic loss for words. "Ada, when this is over and you're ready to go home…"

Her heart clenched, painfully. She didn't want to think about what would happen after she finally made that trip to Dresden. "What?" Her voice sounded breathless and strained, even to her own ears.

"May I accompany you back to New York? I've never been to America."

Ada let out a breath she hadn't realized she was

holding. Excitement over the notion of his visiting America made a smile spread across her face. "Captain Reed needs to take his dirigible over the ocean," she said, thinking of the character she loved so much.

"It's high time he did so. He needs to see New York, Chicago, Niagara Falls. He's been all over Europe and Asia, a few times. He needs to set down roots somewhere new."

That feeling Ada couldn't put a name to rose again, that deep lust she'd felt the first time she saw him, followed by something deeper. *Affection*, she realized. She was very fond of him, could see that growing into something more. And that idea didn't terrify her.

From his words and the look on his face now, Ada suspected he felt the same.

She wanted to show him where she came from, introduce him to her own raucous family. She knew now he wouldn't be appalled at their table manners or simple home.

"I know it's impolite to invite oneself to another's home," Max said.

"We did a lot of impolite things to each other last night and this morning."

Max laughed. "I wouldn't be a bother?"

"Hell, no! Will Captain Reed start hunting vampires, too?"

"Perhaps it's time he takes up a monster-hunting hobby."

Ada's hands slid over his shoulders, bringing his head down to hers for a kiss. He responded immediately, pressing his body against hers so she could feel the full evidence of his arousal. In that instant, there were no Searchers to worry about, no vampire lunatic running through London…

"Oh! I beg your pardon, sir." The study door slammed shut, and Weston's shuffling footsteps sounded across the carpet runner in the corridor.

Max released her, but kept one arm around her waist. "We should find him and apologize," he said. "He's a professional, but can still be scandalized."

"We should also eat some garlic before we go back out," Ada said.

"An excellent excuse for kissing you one last time," Max said. "Although I doubt your smelling and tasting of garlic would put me off." The promising look in his eyes left Ada's knees weak, and she didn't doubt that was true.

Arm still around her waist, he led her to the door. "Besides," he said, "Weston will be scandalized enough once I break off a couple of legs from that ugly table in the library."

THEY STOPPED at a telegraph office on the way to Edward Quinn's likeliest hideout, where Ada sent another cable to the New York branch. Max hired a steam cab to take them to the Searcher office, but no one answered the door when Ada knocked.

"They could be ignoring us or out hunting," she said. She removed a sheet of foolscap and a pencil from her satchel and scribbled a short note, telling them about Edward Quinn and the Knightsbridge address. Before she could fold it and slide it under the front door, Max took it from her and added something.

"What is it?" she asked. His handwriting was impeccable.

"I'm telling them where I live and about my

uncle's belongings," Max said. "When we depart England, I'll leave instructions with Weston to turn over anything from Uncle James's notes that they may find useful. I know you aren't happy with the London branch," he said, noting the way Ada's lip curled in distaste at the mention of Seecombe's outfit. "But they wouldn't be Searchers if they didn't know how to eradicate vampires, would they?"

It was sensible, but didn't irritate Ada any less. "You're right." Ada hated that. The London Searchers were too few in number and there was their backward notion of keeping the group men-only to consider, but they wouldn't have thrived as long as they had without being somewhat competent. Given that she and Max were leaving the country and there was still the matter of vampires roaming London, it was best to turn over Dr. Sterling's notes and journals to the Searchers.

Max hired another steam cab to take them to Lord Greenstone's home. It was fully dark outside when they arrived, and the drapes hanging from the grand house's windows were pulled tightly closed. The garden was still maintained, but aside from that, the house appeared deserted. The gas lamps flanking either side of the door were unlit and no smoke issued from the stone chimney. For all intents and purposes, the home appeared totally unoccupied.

Except that miserable housekeeper at the Halsalls' house, Mrs. Poole, told them otherwise. Edward Quinn was alive. Well, *undead*, Ada mentally corrected herself, and terrorizing London. And he was very likely making his uncle's city home his hiding place.

The upside, she mused, was that Edward

Quinn was a younger vampire, and inexperienced. He should be an easier kill than usual.

She and Max looked over their shoulders, but the street was quiet. Distantly they heard the whistles from steam cabs on the nearest thoroughfare, but there wasn't a vehicle near them otherwise.

"Should we knock?" Max asked.

"You must be new to breaking and entering."

"I'm new to all of this."

"Max, we aren't vampires. We don't have to wait for an invitation." Still, what if there was someone inside? A butler, maybe? Silas Weston cared for Max's house in his absence. Maybe someone cared for Lord Greenstone's. The garden, at least.

But if the only person inside was Edward Quinn…

It was best to break in and have the element of surprise on their side.

"Do you suppose there's a back door?" she asked. "There's no one here right now, but I don't want to draw any attention to us."

"There should be a servants' entrance around the back or side of the house. It's a common feature for homes like this."

They crept away from the front entrance, around the side of the house. True to Max's word, there was a door at the back. The windows on either side of it were just as dark as the ones facing the street.

Ada withdrew a metal file from her satchel and wedged it between the door and jamb. Weathered wood splintered under the file, and it was a tense few seconds before the door gave way on unoiled hinges. Both of them winced. The creak was loud enough to wake the dead.

The house was just as dark inside as out, but Ada could make out an empty counter in the darkness and guessed they were in a kitchen. A strong odor of spoiled food permeated the air, and as her nose tried to process the awful smell, something else hit her.

Pain. Her temples throbbed and pounded in time with her heartbeat. Immediately she felt for the vial of holy water she always kept in her skirt pocket. She then removed her stake and mallet from her satchel, tucking them under her arm. Max saw her do so and quickly had his in hand, too.

"He's in here somewhere," she whispered.

Max didn't reply but tapped his head, looking at her questioningly. "Sense?" he mouthed.

Ada nodded.

They padded through the kitchen on tiptoe, Ada grateful that Max wasn't making an issue of her being in the lead.

Tonight should be simple. Edward Quinn was a new vampire. But she couldn't quell the nervousness that lodged itself in the pit of her stomach, and beneath that, fear.

Ada wasn't afraid of vampires. What brought it on tonight?

She already knew the answer. *Max.* She would never forgive herself if something happened to him.

She removed a small flameless torch from her satchel and switched it on. Its dull yellow light barely illuminated the darkened servants' corridor she and Max crept through, but it was better than nothing.

The house smelled dusty and unused. Its occupants were likely in the country shooting pheasants or whatever dukes did when they weren't in London. But there was something else under the disused smell, something sinister. A faint smell of death that Ada automatically associated with vampires lingered in the air.

Edward Quinn was very close by. She tightened her grip on her stake. A rustle behind her told her Max was probably doing the same.

The servants' corridor led into an empty sitting room. Its fireplace was cold, and when Ada flashed her torch over a table she spotted a half-full bottle of brandy, surrounded by a layer of dust. A squat crystal glass rested next to the bottle, dregs of brandy clinging to the bottom. Who knew how long ago someone drank it?

And was that someone still alive, or undead?

She looked over her shoulder at Max, who kept his stake at the ready. His eyes darted around the room before settling on her face. "He isn't here."

"He is. My head is saying so."

"I mean, he hasn't been in here for weeks. No one has." Max gestured to the ceiling. "We should look upstairs."

"Vampires are likelier to hide in cellars," Ada said.

"If the cellar here is anything like mine, it will be too full of preserves and wine for a vampire to make himself comfortable. I think we should look upstairs first."

It was a sound idea, and Ada didn't know what was usually kept in upper class English cellars. "I'll go first," she said, heading for the doorway. There had to be a staircase nearby that she hasn't spotted yet.

A few steps into the corridor and a left turn had her at the foot of the carpeted stairs. When she shone her torch over the steps, she saw large, muddy footprints dried in the fibers. "Max," she whispered urgently. "Look."

The footprints were large and obviously male, and led upstairs. Ada and Max ascended, their footsteps silent on the carpet.

The landing upstairs branched off in two, much like Max's home. There were more footprints on both sets of stairs, making it impossible to guess where Edward Quinn might be hiding. And he *was* hiding, Ada knew; her headache hadn't ceased. The bastard was in here somewhere.

"Which way?" Max whispered.

"You don't have to bother trying to be quiet," a voice said in the darkness. It was male, had the same cultured accent as Max's, but there was a touch of contempt to his tone. "*I* can hear you plainly."

Heart pounding, Ada dropped her torch and gripped her stake and mallet. Before she could react, light flooded the landing from electric lamps lining the wall. At the top of the stairs to their left stood a black-clad figure, his skin pale and looking almost leathery. A network of scars crisscrossed his face, the result of being attacked with holy water. He was all too familiar to Ada. "*You!*" she gasped.

He was the one who bit her that first night in London, the vampire who swooped out into the night as a bat. Who nearly ripped her throat out.

The vampire sniffed the air, then fixed his bloodshot eyes on Ada. "I thought I recognized you. You're the American dhampir who tried to kill me."

Ada didn't offer a response. She simply lunged for the vampire, managing to knock him off-balance. She didn't have the element of surprise on her side anymore, and she damned herself for not arriving earlier, before he rose for the night. She should have listened to Max and come here earlier in the day. Then she could have staked him while he slept the daylight away.

But there hadn't been time for that; Max needed to be outfitted with weapons, the London branch had to be informed of their activities.

Quinn lurched on his feet, clearly taken aback by Ada's attack. Maybe he thought she would ask questions first, or she could be enthralled long enough for him to try to kill her. Again.

Max jumped into the fray, brandishing his stake and mallet. The vampire deftly stepped away with an inhuman speed. "Why did you kill my uncle?" he said through gritted teeth.

Not now, Max! Ada aimed her stake at the vampire's chest, but only managed to tap it with her mallet before Quinn pushed her away. Still, the action managed to withdraw a hiss of irritation from him.

"I was turned six months ago," Edward Quinn said. "By a vampire in Paris. Lisette said I would love it, and by God she was right." He narrowed his eyes at Ada. "You killed her."

Ada didn't respond. Instead, she withdrew her vial of holy water and flung it at his face.

Quinn screamed, and the sizzle of burning flesh assaulted Ada's senses. She readied her stake again.

"Why did you kill James Sterling and Cerys Hughes?" Max tried again.

Quinn angrily scrubbed at his face with clawed hands, but he answered Max's question. "Cerys? That sniveling maid? She rejected this gift, and

James was helping her." He turned his burned face to Ada. "I know what you're up to."

His eyes flashed red, and his incisors extended past his lips. One pale hand latched to her wrist, twisting until an audible snap sounded and she dropped her stake.

For the first time since she started hunting vampires, Ada screamed.

Fangs latched on to her throat, and a deep, searing pain that she never experienced before shuddered through her body. She tried to push him off her, but her broken wrist wasn't cooperating. She heard a shout that sounded very far away, and her knees buckled. Then all she could hear was the vampire greedily sucking her blood, and the electric lamps illuminating the corridor dimmed as her eyes fell shut.

CHAPTER
EIGHT

Rage colored his vision red. Max launched himself against the vampire, pushing Ada out of the way just enough to hammer his own stake through the monster's chest.

Quinn turned shocked eyes to Max for all of two seconds, before they rolled up in his head and his ruined face turned gray. His grip on Ada slackened as his body disintegrated until he was nothing but a pile of oily ashes inside black clothing.

Max brushed everything aside, gathering Ada in his arms. Her eyes were closed, her face pale and smeared with blood. The blood was not just on her face, he noted with a growing, horrifying realization of what had just happened. Her neck and dress were stained, and more blood flowed from the wound in her throat, so much worse than the one that brought her to his flat a few days ago.

She wasn't moving, and her skin was clammy when he touched her. Her breaths were short and shallow.

"Sterling!"

The yell from the foot of the stairs had his

heart pounding in alarm, but the sight there was one of the best he ever saw. "Seecombe!"

The Searcher had a stake in hand but tossed it aside when he reached the landing and saw Quinn's remains. His eye widened at the sight of Ada in Max's arms. "We have to take her to a doctor," Seecombe said. "She's losing a lot of blood."

Max wrapped his scarf around Ada's neck, but the fabric was quickly saturated. Seecombe pressed his own against the wound and helped lift Ada into Max's arms. "I have a steam cab waiting nearby," he said. "She needs immediate attention." Worry creased his features.

"She needs blood," Max said hoarsely.

"You're speaking of a transfusion. That's far too risky."

Ada's breathing grew more labored, and Max knew she didn't have much time. "I think it's the only chance she has," he said, damning the break in his voice.

"We have physicians available. They'll be able to help." Seecombe was already on the stairs, and Max quickly followed. He held tightly to Ada.

Do not die on me. I need you too much.

He and Seecombe dashed for a battered steam cab one street over, and Seecombe slid into the driver's seat. The vehicle hissed as it started and a peculiar rattle sounded through it, but Max didn't care. "You received our note?" he asked.

"I did," Seecombe replied tersely.

"My late uncle did a great amount of research into blood, including transfusions. There may be something useful for your physician to help him. James's butler will give him everything he needs."

"I don't think we have time for that," Seecombe said. He jerked the steam cab into traffic and brought it to full speed, far faster than Max had ever experienced before. His stomach lurched in protest, but he didn't let go of Ada.

Her eyes opened briefly and she stared at him, recognition briefly flashing through them. Just as quickly, she sighed a little and closed them again.

"Ada," Max said sharply. "Wake up!"

Her eyes remained closed, but she was still breathing, thank God. Max kept the scarves pressed against her neck and his eyes on her face.

"Please," he added, his voice softer.

It wasn't fair. He finally met an amazing woman, someone who was strong and smart and warm, someone he could see himself actually falling in love with, and he was in grave danger of losing her. Max wasn't ordinarily petulant and decried the entitled members of his class who felt the world owed them everything simply because of their ancestry, but this time, faced with this potential loss, he was angry. He would destroy every vampire he ever came across, make it his life's work, if she died tonight.

And if she didn't, Max was determined to remain at her side, helping rid the world of monsters. It was time to stop gallivanting around Europe and Asia, finding fodder for the character he created to live through vicariously, and start really living. Work toward something for the greater good, rather than massaging his own ego. Make a positive change in the world he had taken so much from and had so much handed directly to him, without his deserving it.

"How much longer until we reach your headquarters?" he asked tersely.

"At top speeds, twelve minutes," Seecombe said. "How is she faring?"

"She's still breathing."

"Important, but not enough."

"She needs that doctor."

"He'll be there," Seecombe promised. "There are two physicians in the London Searchers."

Ada stirred, but didn't open her eyes. Her breath shuddered, and for a horrifying moment Max thought she might die in his arms. But she exhaled, and her shallow breaths continued.

He held her to him and silently prayed.

ADA WAS IMMEDIATELY TAKEN from him and placed on a makeshift examination table as soon as they reached the Searcher headquarters. A tall, slim man who reminded Max of his Uncle James introduced himself as Pilcher, the organization's physician.

"She's losing blood rapidly," Pilcher said. "That vampire was determined to kill her."

"It was the second time he bit her," Max said.

Pilcher inspected the wound, a needle in hand for stitches. "He had an axe to grind, and his teeth hit something vital." Without missing a beat, he immediately soaked a rag in holy water and pressed it to her neck. She moaned, and her eyes briefly blinked open before closing again. It was clear she hadn't seen anyone in the room. Pilcher cleaned the bite as best he could before he started to stitch it closed. The sutures would leave a noticeable scar, but Max didn't care about that. He doubted Ada would, either.

"But she can be healed? You can do that?" Max heard the pleading in his voice but didn't care.

123

"She needs stitches and blood." Worry creased Pilcher's face. "Without it, she likely won't last the rest of the night. I'm surprised she's made it this long."

"Do you know how to do a transfusion?" Max asked.

"I've attended some experimental transfusion therapies, but it's still a very risky procedure."

"How many?"

"I beg your pardon?"

"How many transfusions have you attended?"

Pilcher paused for a second. Max saw doubt flit across the man's face. "Five," he finally said. "I observed four and participated in one."

"How many patients lived?"

Pilcher hesitated again before replying. "Three. We lost two. We still don't understand why that occurred. There are theories relating to serology and why some patients thrive after a transfusion from another patient and others die, but we're still unable to understand exactly why only some procedures are successful."

"You said she's going to die unless she receives blood," Max said.

"I did. There's a slim chance she may survive, but it isn't high. Her color is terrible and her pulse is slowing. She's lost too much." Pilcher gestured to Max. For the first time, he looked down at his clothing and saw the stains there, felt blood sticking to his skin. He hadn't noticed it, nor did he care.

He was soaked in it. He hadn't realized there was so much inside one person.

"What if I gave her blood?" Max asked. "You know how to do the procedure, do you not?"

"I do, but I don't have the equipment on hand."

Max's mind raced. "My uncle's home does. Is there someone who can go there and retrieve it? His butler will help in any way possible."

"It's inadvisable to bring someone else here tonight," Pilcher said.

"My uncle died by Edward Quinn's hand," Max said. "He knew about the existence of vampires and was conducting research into a cure. His butler knows about them, too."

Pilcher's lips thinned. "I'll perform the procedure if the equipment can be brought here immediately. Speak to Seecombe, and he will make the arrangements." The doctor's expression softened. "I can see Miss Burgess is dear to you. Do you understand the gravity of what you're offering? This transfusion may kill her."

"If I don't do it, that vampire bite will."

Pilcher considered this as he continued stitching Ada's wound. She didn't flinch at the needle piercing her flesh. The doctor may as well have been sewing a child's toy. Her broken wrist hung limply off the edge of the table.

"I'll do it," Pilcher finally said. "As soon as the necessary apparatus is brought to me."

SILAS WESTON ACCOMPANIED Seecombe back to the Searcher headquarters, a blindfold across his eyes. "What is the meaning of this?" Max demanded.

Seecombe removed the blindfold, and Weston blinked at the brightness of the room. "I told you I wasn't planning to reveal your secrets," the butler said indignantly. "God knows I've kept enough. What's one more?" He flinched at the sight of Ada, so pale and still on the examination table. But she was still breathing, Max noted to himself.

A large case was gripped in Weston's hands. "Who shall I give the transfusion apparatus to?"

Pilcher took it and opened it. "It's immaculately clean," he said, removing the metal pump and needles resembling railroad spikes. Max looked away. He didn't want to think about the massive needles piercing his veins until he had to.

But it would be worth it, if his blood saved Ada.

"Of course it is," Weston said. "Both my late employer and myself kept everything in that house and his practice spotless."

"Of course he did. I apologize." To Max, Pilcher said, "You're certain about this?"

Max nodded and stripped off his shirt.

"Lie on that divan," Pilcher said, pointing to the well-worn piece of furniture in the corner. "I won't lie to you, Mr. Sterling, this is going to be painful. Would you care for a dram?"

Max took a deep breath and forced himself to look away from the transfusion equipment. "Scottish whiskey, if you have it."

"That can be arranged." Pilcher called for Seecombe, who quickly produced a bottle and glass. Max knocked back a couple of fingers of the whiskey, but the fiery liquid didn't quell his nerves.

Pilcher held up one spiked needle. His hand trembled slightly, and Max had an unsettling feeling that the doctor was nervous. But his voice was steady when he spoke again. "Let's begin."

CHAPTER
NINE

H er throat was raw. *Water. I need water.*
Water sounded good right about now.
Maybe it would help with the nausea.

Water and a blanket. And a proper bed, something better than the board she had to be lying on right now. Even her modest accommodations on the steamship to Dresden were better than this, and she shared a room with three other travelers on that voyage.

She licked her lips, tried to speak. But her throat was too dry, and her voice wouldn't work. Her wrist screamed in pain when she tried to shift her position.

No matter. She would go back to sleep, and when she woke up, she would get that glass of water and a blanket.

∾

"She's waking up."

"She woke up before, and went right back to sleep."

Ada heard the rustling of fabric and Max's

voice, and forced herself to open her eyes. Her voice was barely more than a croak when she tried to speak. "Where am I?"

Max sat on a chair beside whatever uncomfortable bed she lay in, face pale and drawn. An unfamiliar man sat next to him. "Excellent," the man said. "Your color is much improved, and from my examinations you seem capable of making a recovery. But you'll never have the full use of your left hand again, I doubt."

"Recovery?" she said in a small voice.

She remembered Edward Quinn's flashing red eyes, the terrifying realization that she was going to die when her stake missed him again, and the son of a bitch jumped at her, fangs sharp.

She hadn't staked him. She failed. But she was still alive. She knew she was. She would not be in this much pain if she died, so what the hell happened?

"Quinn," she said. "What happened to him?"

"I staked the bastard," Max said.

Ada forced herself to sit up, wincing at the striations of pain from her set and bandaged wrist. At least her wrist was still attached and the doctor hadn't amputated anything. Max quickly rose and helped her. A wave of nausea crested over her and her head protested the move, but she took deep breaths until the feelings passed. "Your first kill," she said, forcing levity into her voice. "Maximilian, I'm proud of you." She felt something stiff wrapped around her neck and raised her hand to it, feeling the bandages there. "Oh, damn. Not again."

"How do you feel?" asked the other man, speaking for the first time.

"Like I've been in a hell of a fight with a vampire and lost, which is exactly what happened."

"You received a transfusion of blood from Max," the man said. "Three days ago."

"What?" Ada didn't know which was more alarming: that she received and survived a transfusion, or that she slept away three days.

"You would have died without it," he said.

That bit of news didn't surprise Ada. "Who are you?" she asked, sidestepping his explanation.

"George Pilcher. I'm a physician and Searcher. Seecombe and Sterling brought you here after you were attacked by the vampire you were hunting."

"And you gave me some of Max's blood," she said.

"I don't know if you're aware of the risks of transfusion, but you and Max are a successful case," Pilcher said. "It's a pity I won't be able to write about this for a journal."

Ada didn't care about journals. She was alive, albeit she still felt terrible. But that would pass.

"Edward Quinn is dead," she said slowly. "Truly dead this time."

"I didn't expect to stake him myself," Max said. "But now that it's over and you're going to recover, I'm glad I did. It won't erase what he did to James or Cerys Hughes, but at least he can't turn more people. Or eat them."

"It's a never-ending cycle, Max," Ada said. "I told you they're clever bastards. Help me out of bed?"

Max lifted her off the bed, which she saw now was nothing more than a table. No wonder she was so uncomfortable. Her makeshift bed and the bandages around her neck and wrist made for a stiff body. When she tried to stretch her muscles, she found that she still wore her corset, and her dress was bloodstained and smelled of sweat. She added a bath to the list of things she wanted immediately.

But the item at the top of that list was right in front of her, the lines of worry erasing from his features as he gazed down at her, whole and healthy. Or almost healthy.

"I want to go home," she said.

The words escaped her before she could think them through. She was thousands of miles from home, an ocean away from it. But she wasn't thinking of New York. Home was wherever Max would be.

His eyes lit up with understanding. "Let's go, then."

∽

SEECOMBE WAS KIND ENOUGH to take them home in his battered steam cab, a vehicle, he explained, that served the Searchers very well. It managed to get her and Max back to the London headquarters, helping to save her life.

She owed the London branch a debt she didn't think she could repay. She disliked being a novelty to them, but the dislike she harbored after initially meeting them had let up a little. She would never fully thaw to their antiquated ways of running the Searchers, but they did know what they were doing.

Weston had a maid arrange a bath for her as soon as he laid eyes on her, and sent another one to a shop to replace her clothing. She removed her ruined dress as soon as she could, mindful of her broken wrist. She left her clothing, including her undergarments, in a pile in her bedchamber's fireplace. She gingerly removed the bandage circling her neck, gaping in the room's polished looking glass at the black sutures holding the vampire bite closed. It was bad, the worst she'd ever had, and it would leave a noticeable scar that no amount of holy water could remove.

Edward Quinn hadn't meant to just drain her. He wanted to make her suffer. And in those terrifying moments before she lost consciousness, she remembered feeling the worst pain she ever experienced. The fear had been paralyzing and all-encompassing, nothing she'd ever felt before. But that attack only served to strengthen her resolve to continue her work.

Vampires must not flourish.

She stepped into a bath as soon as she could, relishing the feel of hot water washing away dried blood and sweat, working carefully around the bandages on her wrist. She dunked her head under the water, scrubbing her hair with soap using her uninjured hand. It smelled fresh and masculine, like Max.

A knock sounded on the door. When she popped her head back up, the object of her thoughts had opened her bedchamber door a crack and peeked in.

"You don't have to knock," she said, stretching out in the water. She crossed her ankles and perched her feet on the edge of the tub. "I think we're beyond the knocking stage. Come on in."

He did, and she noticed how his eyes raked over her naked form. He sat on the bed, watching her.

"I could use help scrubbing my back," she said, holding the soap out to him with her free hand.

She sat up straight and pushed her wet hair out

of the way. Max fished her washcloth out of the water and massaged her back, his strokes slow and sure.

"How are you feeling?" he asked.

"Like I'm going to live. It's a good feeling to have." She turned around to face him. "Max, I can never thank you enough for saving my life back there. Twice, really." She stretched out her legs, mindful not to splash water to the floor. The hammered brass bathtub was deep, but not so much that she wanted to ruin the carpets.

"I think I was more frightened of the blood transfusion than I was of Edward Quinn," Max said.

"I'm really glad I wasn't awake when you had to make that decision," she said.

"You would have died without it." His voice cracked, and a part of Ada wanted to cry with him. Why, she wasn't sure. They made it out of Lord Greenstone's house alive, with his vampire nephew destroyed. Objective complete, with the only casualty the one they were supposed to kill.

"I could have died if you hadn't. How are *you* feeling, what with losing some blood of your own?"

"I was tired and unsteady for the first day," he said. "I've been eating a great deal of liver on the advice of Dr. Pilcher. He wanted me to drink cow or pig's blood to replace my own more quickly, but I refused. Liver is barely palatable as it is." Max resumed washing her back. "I only started feeling like myself again this morning. I'm unsure how much blood Pilcher took."

"And no one knows why your blood worked," she said. Her medical knowledge was slim. Everything she knew about bloodletting and transfusions came from what she and Max read in James's journals.

"It was a lucky shot in the dark. Pilcher said if the transfusion failed, you wouldn't be here now." Max set down the washcloth. "Do you need any more help bathing?"

There was a teasing, suggestive note to Max's voice, and it reassured Ada. She needed the levity, to feel a little more normal again. "No," she said. "But I'll need help drying off."

A low chuckle was his only reply, and she stood up, water sluicing over her body. Max had towels ready and wrapped her up, lifting her out of the water. He deposited her on the bed, and she flushed, remembering what happened the last time he was there.

Judging from his dilated pupils and half-hooded eyelids, she knew he was thinking about the same thing. "You can't tie me to the bedpost this time," she said, looking at her injured wrist.

"Some other time, then."

"Maybe I'll tie *you* to the posts."

"A situation I'm amenable to in the future, but not today." He lay down next to her on his side, levering himself up on one arm to face her. That tired, drawn look he had been wearing since she woke up was fading, but he was still pale, and she suspected he might be weaker from blood loss than he was letting on.

He traced her lips with his thumb, the motion stoking a flame that reminded her that not all of her body parts were injured in the fight with Edward Quinn. She broke the short distance between them and kissed him, her good hand running through his hair.

She broke the kiss, pushing away her towel and

sitting up. She fumbled with his shirt's buttons one-handed.

"Ada?" Max's voice was hesitant. "We don't have to do this if you're not feeling well."

"I feel fine." Maybe it was her near-death experience, maybe she would just never get enough of Maximilian Sterling, but she needed him now. Unless... "Are *you* not feeling up to this?"

"Are you mad?" He lightly nipped her ear. "I always am."

He helped her with his shirt buttons, then his trousers. He was breathing as heavily as she was. Anticipation coiled low in her belly, a spring ready to launch. When his mouth found one nipple and gently bit it, a moan of pleasure escaped her.

He ran his hand over her broken wrist, fingertips skimming the bandages. "Thank you for not letting them cut off my hand," Ada said.

"There wasn't a bone sticking out, so there wasn't a need for it. Is it bothering you?"

"No." Her left hand was her staking hand, her right always held the mallet. She knew it would be a little while before she could go back out hunting vampires again.

Max's fingers laced through those of her uninjured hand as he bent over her. His erection pressed against her belly, teasing her. The memory of their last time together in bed was at the front of her mind, her body demanding release.

"Now," she said impatiently.

He dragged his cock against her skin, further inflaming her senses. "You're always going to be demanding in bed, aren't you? Begging me, pleading, demanding..."

"Yes," she said, arching an eyebrow at him. "I suggest you get used to it." She hooked her legs around his hips, urging him closer to her body. "Max, please."

He obliged her, sliding into her body in one smooth stroke. Without any further urging from Ada, he picked up a rhythm that had her panting, already closer to the edge than she thought possible.

Her orgasm ripped through her, her cry muffled by Max's lips crashing down on hers. Still not sated, another wave of climax washed over her, and Max's rapid breathing told her he was close, too. He pulled out, and she immediately reached between their bodies, stroking his cock through his own orgasm.

They were silent for a few minutes, entwined in each other's bodies, with only the sound of their breathing in the room.

"How's your wrist?" Max finally asked.

It twinged, but it wasn't unbearable. Ada hadn't thought about it at all until Max mentioned it. "It's fine. Do you think the bath water is still warm?"

He stood up, pushing the damp towel off the bed. He gathered her in his arms and she let out a delighted squeal. "Perhaps. Let's get in."

CHAPTER
TEN

Ada had never traveled in first class accommodations aboard a dirigible before, and her excitement at the available amenities would never cease to delight Max. She repeatedly told him that their trip to Dresden was everything she wanted it to be, and more. She found the cemetery where some of her dhampir ancestors rested—unstaked, she was sure to remind him—to pay her respects, and they stayed for ten leisurely days at a lovely hotel with automated bathtubs. There wasn't any staff lugging water buckets to their room, a convenience Max wanted more of.

And nary a vampire to be found in Dresden, at least according to Ada and her sensory ability. Still, they both carried stakes with them when they took in the city's nightlife.

Now, they stood on the dirigible's upper deck, watching the waves of the Atlantic Ocean crash a hundred feet below their vessel. They had eight hours or so before they made dock in New York City, after which Max was going to meet Ada's family. She told him about her brothers, about the townhouse they all shared in the heart of the city, about the Searcher headquarters there. She sent cables to the rest of the Burgess clan and the vampire hunters, and their replies told of a friendly group of people looking forward to meeting him.

"What are you thinking about?" Ada asked him. Her unruly russet hair was tightly pulled back in a bun at the nape of her neck, but strands escaped to whip around her face in the wind.

"You." It was the truth, but there was more to it. He had been thinking about something else for a few days, and was unsure how to bring it up. *There's no time like the present*, he told himself. "Actually, I was thinking about the time you told me you wanted to be a pilot."

"I wanted that a long time ago."

"But if you had the opportunity now, would you resume your lessons?"

Her eyes widened. "It's not practical at this point, Max."

"But if you could, would you?"

"Yes," she said, without any hesitation. "Immediately. Having a dirigible at my disposal would be a godsend, both for hunting vampires around the country and my own desire. I've always loved flying."

"Would you accept an offer of lessons at the Air Academy?"

She froze, lips a perfect round O of shock.

"I'd like to accompany you, of course, once I complete training with the Searchers and I know my vampire kills aren't flukes of luck."

"Max, it's a generous offer," she said, but he continued on.

"It wouldn't just be for you," he said. "Captain Reed needs his adventures in America, and he needs a lady pilot to accompany him sometimes."

"So pilot lessons for me would benefit you," she said, but she was smiling now. Smiling, but there was a light film of tears in her eyes that had nothing to do with the wind whipping around them.

"Greatly."

"Oh, God, Max, it's such a generous offer," she said, bringing gloved hands to her mouth.

"Say yes," he urged her. "I want you to have this. For you, and to help save the world from monsters."

"Okay." She took in a shaky breath of salt-tinged air. "When we get settled in New York, we'll call on the Academy," she said. She wiped tears from her eyes and threw her arms around Max, squeezing him with a strength that belied her size. "Thank you," she said, her voice muffled by his overcoat.

He stroked her hair. "You're very much welcome. I wanted to give you a gift you would enjoy."

"But the trip…"

"The Dresden holiday was to make up for the time you lost staking vampires. This is different. I doubt you would enjoy a gift of jewelry or furs as much."

She sniffled. "No, probably not."

His arms tightened around her. "I love you, Ada. I want you to have the opportunities you need to continue our work."

Her gaze held his. "I love you too, Max."

It was the first time either said those words, but he knew it wouldn't be the last.

"You're going to be a fine Searcher," she said.

He leaned down to kiss her. "As long as I'm with you."

ABOUT THE AUTHOR

Jessica Marting is a sci-fi and paranormal romance author, art enthusiast (not quite an artist, despite all that time in art school), an avid reader, and makeup collector. She lives in Toronto.

Sign up for her newsletter at jessicamarting.com/newsletter for pre-order alerts, sales, freebies, and more.

ALSO BY JESSICA MARTING

Magic & Mechanicals

Wolf's Lady

Sea Change

Bound in Blood

Dragon's Keep

Spellbound

Zone Cyborgs

Haven

Paradise

Oasis

Safe Harbor

Sanctuary

Refuge

The Commons

Supernova

Celestial Chaos

Standalone Novels & Novellas

Spindle's End

Trade Secrets

Neon Vice

Dead Ringer

Escape From Europa 10

Castaways
Demon's Favor

9 781989 780251